"Silky?

"If the idea of massaging me is to help me forget the pain in my calf, it's working. If you've got something more than a massage in mind, just say so."

She frowned, confused not only by what he was saying, but by the husky way he was saying it. Dropping her gaze, she was shocked to see that she'd unconsciously massaged her way up his leg until her fingers were barely beneath the edge of his shorts.

"Oh!" She jerked her hands away. "I'm sorry. My mind must have been wandering."

His lips parted in a grin ripe with charming menace. "Mine definitely was. Do you want to know where?"

RENEE ROSZEL

was born and lives in Tulsa, Oklahoma with her husband and two sons. She covers both physical as well as mental exercise by alternating her writing with teaching a class in Rhythmic Aerobics. She enjoys the two aspects of her work enormously, and says, "It's great to be paid for things you'd do for free!"

Dear Reader:

Romance readers have been enthusiastic about Silhouette Special Editions for years. And that's not by accident: Special Editions were the first of their kind and continue to feature realistic stories with heightened romantic tension.

The longer stories, sophisticated style, greater sensual detail and variety that made Special Editions popular are the same elements that will make you want to read book after book.

We hope that you enjoy this Special Edition today, and will enjoy many more.

The Editors at Silhouette Books

RENEE ROSZEL
Wind Shadow

Silhouette Special Edition

Published by Silhouette Books New York

America's Publisher of Contemporary Romance

Silhouette Books by Renee Roszel

Wild Flight (D #90)
Wind Shadow (SE #207)

SILHOUETTE BOOKS, a Division of Simon & Schuster, Inc.
1230 Avenue of the Americas, New York, N.Y. 10020

Copyright © 1984 by Renee Roszel
Cover artwork copyright © 1984 Robert Maguire

Distributed by Pocket Books

ISBN: 0-671-53707-5

First Silhouette Books printing December, 1984

10 9 8 7 6 5 4 3 2 1

All of the characters in this book are fictitious. Any resemblance to actual persons, living or dead, is purely coincidental.

Map by Ray Lundgren

To the wind
and his lengthening shadows

Doug
Doug and Randy

Wind Shadow

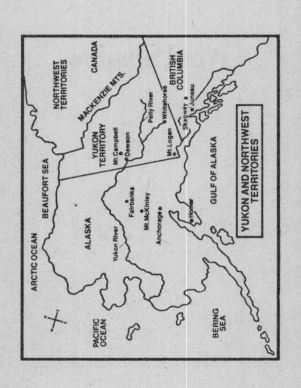

YUKON AND NORTHWEST TERRITORIES

Chapter One

Silky dropped onto the tall stool behind the Emergency Admitting desk and shook her head, her lips parted in a wry smile. The giggle that bubbled in her throat drew Nurse Page's curious glance away from a seemingly endless stream of paperwork. "What's so funny?" the older woman asked.

Silky pushed a loose wisp of corn-silk hair back up into the tight knot at her nape. "What people do to each other in the name of love." She shrugged, her green eyes twinkling. "You were busy when this young couple came in—the man had actually *glued* himself to his girl friend."

"What?" The chubby nurse's mouth gaped open and her ballpoint clattered unnoticed to the floor. "For heaven's sake, why?"

Silky shrugged helplessly. "Well, the woman was pretty upset, having to come down here in a taxi with a man's hands glued to her shoulders, so I'm not sure I got all the facts." She had to stop talking and stifle the urge to smile as she recalled the scene. It certainly hadn't been funny to the people involved. She tried again. "Apparently she'd told her boyfriend that she was moving out, and he didn't take it very well."

Nurse Page exploded with laughter. "Apparently!" She snorted derisively. "And I thought I'd seen everything Anchorage had to offer in my fifteen years here at Midtown. Say"—she looked up at Silky as she tossed the tissue away—"why don't you get me the girl's name? After breaking up with a crazy guy like that, I bet she'd love to meet my brother—bum that he is. I've never known him to be much into glue, so maybe he's got *something* going for him."

"Oh, Betty, your brother can't be as bad as you make him out to be."

The older woman brightened, her drab blue eyes bigger but no less drab through the thick lenses of her glasses. "Well then, Silky, why don't you just let me give the bum—I mean my darling baby brother—*your* number?"

Silky laughed. This type of conversation wasn't new for her. Ever since she'd come to work at Midtown as an emergency medical technician eight months ago, it seemed as though everyone here, from the head of thoracic surgery to the high school boy who swept up, had a brother, cousin, "close" friend or misunderstood son they wanted to fix her up with. She shook her head and pulled a hefty textbook out from under the desk. "Thanks, Betty, but no. I'm not dating right now. I have enough to think about just trying to graduate." She tapped the book with a neatly trimmed nail. "And I've got a final tomorrow."

Betty looked down at the book. "Another one? You must never sleep, working here all night and going to college all day."

Silky smiled, but didn't look up as she flipped through the pages. "Just afternoons. And this is my last exam."

"Good. Then you can take over this monster of a hospital and run it right."

Silky tilted her head toward Betty. "Well, the degree is in hospital management, but the job I've been offered here is as an assistant administrator. It's a pretty long jump from that to running the place."

"Well, it's a darn sight closer to it than any other woman around here has gotten. Mark my words, someday you'll run this sterile barn, and we'll all be the better for it." She thumped Silky's back a little harder than one might expect from an angel of mercy, and Silky had to catch herself on the desk edge to keep from slipping. Unfortunately, she caught herself with her stomach. "Thanks . . ." She coughed weakly.

The phone flashed silently for attention, and

Nurse Page lifted the receiver, oblivious. Silky flipped through her text to the test material and breathed deeply.

The receiver clicked into its cradle as Betty lowered her plump torso from her stool. "The workup that Dr. Hooper wanted is ready. Will you be okay for a while? I'd like to take my break before I come back."

"Sure. What else could happen tonight? It's"— she glanced down at her watch—"3:45."

Scurrying away, Betty quipped over her shoulder, "All the body-gluers are probably asleep by now."

Silky smiled, without looking up. Maybe now she'd be able to study. This test was the final obstacle to be hurdled in a year of tough obstacles.

Glue. Her mind wandered. Maybe she should have tried glue when Rex told her that he was leaving her for someone else. Closing her eyes, she exhaled slowly. After six years of marriage, she had been dropped—tossed out like sour milk —at twenty-seven, a failure at her marriage. Yes, she certainly knew how the man with the glue had felt to have someone he loved tell him that she was going away. It was no laughing matter. Of course, to glue himself to this woman was a crazy, irrational act, but Silky knew that love rarely brings out the most logical, sound thinking in people.

Deep in her thoughts, she hadn't noticed the familiar whoosh of the sliding emergency doors opening, until a low moan and muffled thud brought her head up sharply.

Just inside the door, leaning heavily against the wall, was a young police officer. He was ghostly pale. Blood was oozing from a hole in his blue-uniformed shoulder, and his boyish face was twisted in anguish.

Silky jumped from her stool and rushed to lead the man to a chair. "Here, let me look at that," she offered quietly, gingerly moving the fabric away from his wound to examine it.

He groaned, pounding his fist on his knee. "*Damn* me!"

Silky jumped at his vehemence. "Try to be still. You've lost some blood. You don't want to make it worse by moving around, do you?" She straightened. "It's a clean wound. If I help you, I think you can make it down the hall to a treatment room."

He didn't seem to hear her. His teeth bared in a pained expression, he half-growled, half-sobbed, "I let the guy get my gun! How could I have been so stupid!" He spat the words out in self-disgust, slumping forward weakly.

Alarmed, Silky tried to calm him by taking one of his tightly fisted hands into both of hers. She kept her voice as steady as she could. "Please, it'll be all right—just—"

"All right? *All right*?" he repeated in a high-pitched moan. "The lieutenant'll have my head for this—he went off after the guy on foot."

Silky had to get this man into treatment.

Sighing deeply, she bent and slid an arm about him, coaxing him to his feet. "Come with me. Don't think about it."

He stood shakily, leaning heavily against her. Taking much of his weight, Silky's slender five-feet, seven-inch, 120-pound frame nearly buckled at the knees. Though the policeman couldn't have been over five feet, ten inches tall, he was very weak, and not much more ambulatory than a 150-pound bag of hospital mashed potatoes.

He turned watery gray eyes to her and whispered hoarsely, "Call headquarters. Get help for the lieutenant. . . . He was just a block east of here."

She nodded reassuringly. "Yes—yes, I will." The ashen-faced officer was mumbling incoherently when Dr. Hooper and Betty Page pushed through the door of the treatment room. Silky had removed his jacket and shirt and was cleansing the wound when they took over. As she slipped out to return to her desk, Silky could hear the officer's rasping plea. "Remember, call . . ."

When she reached the desk, she knew the call wouldn't be necessary. Entering the emergency doors were two men, handcuffed together. Both of them looked as though they were in their mid-thirties, and both were mud-spattered, but aside from that, they were poles apart in appearance.

The lieutenant had obviously gotten his man, and Silky breathed a sigh of relief. As they moved toward her, Silky could see that the lieutenant was very angry. His round, ruddy face was set in a deep scowl, and his scalp, beneath thinning brown hair, was as red as his face. He was breathing very heavily. He looked very much the typical police officer in his gray, three-piece suit, white shirt, striped tie and black, wing-tip shoes. He had "conservative, law enforcement officer" written all over his slightly paunchy frame.

And then there was the criminal. He was limping badly, probably injured in the scuffle that got him captured. He was taller than the lieutenant, maybe six-feet, two, and his decidedly uneven gait gave his extremely dark coloring and powerfully broad build the disquieting and unsavory quality of a stalking Alaskan grizzly. His black eyes were coal hard and slitted, and the dark stubble on his craggy jaw spoke as much of his ne'er-do-well lifestyle as did the ancient sweatshirt and worn jeans that clung to his muscular frame. He didn't look like a man easily caught, especially while wielding a gun. The lieutenant was either a very resourceful man or a very lucky one. Silky didn't envy him his job.

Job. Silky steeled herself, shuddering inwardly. This, after all, was a hospital, and she had a job to do, too. The lieutenant had obviously brought this wounded bear of a man here for treatment. She forced herself to move, walking rather stiffly to meet them.

The criminal surprised her by starting to speak. "I need—"

Silky cut in, not wanting to have any more to do with him than absolutely necessary. "Yes, I see. Please sit down and I'll take a look." Without stopping, she motioned them to two chairs near the wall. "I was just about to call headquarters when you came in." Kneeling, she took the muddy hem of the limping man's jeans before looking up into the lieutenant's glowering face. The despair in the young officer's eyes flashed across her mind.

"Before you say anything, I think there is something you should know." She began automatically rolling up the pant leg, trying to form her words carefully. "When someone is injured, his mental state can be extremely important to the speed of his recovery." She watched for some sign of softening in the ruddy glare, but saw none. Swallowing, she forged on, lowering her eyes to the pant leg before her. "It would help if I could tell that young officer who was shot that—that you don't blame him for what happened." She paused hopefully, tilting her face back up. "He's going to be all right, but I think it would help."

"The kid got what he deserved, and you can tell him I said so." The ruddy-faced man's guttural snarl shocked Silky. Stunned, she could only stare up at the unfeeling man. How could he be so callous toward a less-experienced fellow officer?

She swallowed hard. "You can't really mean that. Everyone makes mistakes."

He made a very impolite noise. Feeling highly embarrassed and angry, Silky swallowed the urge to say anything else. Lowering her eyes, she pursed her lips, trying to concentrate solely on her job. Focusing on the injured man's calf, she was surprised to see that it was massively scarred. Very tentatively, she touched the lightly furred leg. The muscles were rock hard.

He hadn't been injured in the chase, as Silky had originally assumed, but was limping because of some previous injury—a bad one. The attempted escape must have been too much of a strain on the healing tissue. She shook her head. "Well, there really isn't much I can do for you—" She moved her gaze to the handcuffed prisoner's face. Every word, every coherent thought left her brain like a scattering of bats fleeing a collapsing belfry.

The black eyes were no longer narrowed in a frown, but twinkling with humor. His lips, fuller than she'd first thought, were lifted in a half-smile. The unexpected masculine allure of his softened features left her oddly paralyzed there, on her knees, with her hands resting on his calf.

He broke the strangely disabling spell, his baritone voice tinged with laughter. "Thank you for your interest in my leg. . . ." He moved his free hand down to tilt the badge that was pinned on the breast of her greens. "Mrs. Silvia Kay

Overbridge." Removing his finger, he shifted his weight to pull a wallet from his hip pocket. "Let me introduce myself." Flipping it open to display a badge and a laminated identification card, he went on, "I'm Lieutenant Banning, Anchorage Detective Division. I'm here to check on Officer Taylor and to get the patrol car keys." His smile was teasing. "I'm glad to hear that he's doing well, and I'll certainly keep in mind what you said about his recovery." Slipping his wallet back into his hip pocket, he extended his free hand, helping her to her feet. "And don't worry about my leg. I know what to do for it."

She felt her face burn with humiliation as she pulled her hand from his larger one and she carefully avoided his eyes.

He spoke again. "I'd appreciate it, Mrs. Overbridge, if you'd check on those keys."

Feeling like a complete dolt, and knowing that Lieutenant Banning would have a good laugh at her expense when he repeated the story later, she mumbled something that she hoped sounded like polite leave-taking, pivoted rigidly on her soft-soled loafers and rushed down the hall.

Silky returned the keys by way of Nurse Page. She never, *never*, wanted to look into those dark, laughing eyes again. What she did want to do was take her break and forget the whole embarrassing mess, but it didn't work. Every time she looked down into her coffee cup, she saw the lazily twinkling, liquid eyes of a man who no doubt thought of her as an idiot. And for some strange reason, that knowledge troubled her much more than it should have.

"Why so quiet?" Annie asked as she and Silky led their heavily loaded ten-speed bicycles through the milling crowd of brightly dressed bikers.

Silky turned toward her apartment-mate, Annie Toone. Slim to the point of boniness, Annie was to most people as charming as a growling Doberman. But to Silky, Annie was a loyal, if not totally lovable, friend. Silky's smile, as she looked at the thirty-one-year-old woman, was more than a little doubtful. "I was just wondering when the men with the padded van are going to come and take me away." She shook her head, her fine blond hair flapping playfully back and forth across her shoulders in long pig-tails. "Annie, what ever possessed me to agree to this madness of yours—a four-week bicycle trip! Am I completely crazy?"

Annie cocked her head toward Silky, her tight red curls barely moving with the strong breeze. "Thanks for that vote of confidence in my sanity, Silk, but remember, I actually got married twice! Now that's nuts!" Annie wrinkled her freckled nose. "But allow me to refresh your memory. First"—she lifted her index finger—"you really need a vacation, and you can't afford to take an around-the-world cruise. Right?"

"Right," Silky agreed reluctantly.

"Second, your new job doesn't open up at Midtown for another five weeks, and with me gone, you'd go crackers all alone in that apartment. Check?"

"Well, actually, Annie—"

"Oh, just say 'check' and *hush!*"

"Check," Silky repeated obediently as Annie hurried on.

"Okay. If you'll remember, you resisted those logical reasons. I knew you would." She lifted her sharp little chin with pretended smugness. "We exceptionally fine salesmen of the world have to be part psychologist, so that we'll know how to appeal to the soft touches of the world— make 'em putty in our hands."

Silky nodded, her eyes narrowing suspiciously. "I'm putty for you, I suppose."

"Silly putty, my dear." Annie's expression became not too pleasantly knowing, and Silky felt uneasy about having started this conversation.

"So, I slugged you in your emotional underbelly with the news that Rex the wonder-louse was coming along on this trip, and—POW!—what an about-face you did! Silky Overbridge was ready to hit the road with the rubber. Remember now?"

Silky cleared her throat self-consciously. "It's coming back to me. What do you say we just drop it—"

"If you want my opinion," Annie interrupted, holding up a hand to halt Silky's attempted protest, "and you should whether you know it or not, just because that pickle-brain broke up with his floozy doesn't mean you have to take him back. You'd do yourself a big favor if you'd just stomp him like you would any other crawling pest. But"—Annie lifted her thin shoulders in exaggerated helplessness and sighed heavily—"it's your life to ruin if you must."

They stopped to let a pair of bikers pedal across their path. Silky shot Annie a perturbed glance. She didn't want to go into this again, especially in public. Trying to keep the conversation from taking an argumentative turn, Silky asked with hard-won control, "Considering how you feel about Rex, I can't understand why you wanted me to come along on this trip."

Annie's high-pitched chuckle sounded a little like a cackle. "Two reasons. First, if absence makes the heart grow fonder, I'm wondering what four weeks of dust and bugs are going to do for you two."

"And second?" Silky demanded tonelessly.

Annie smirked, shaking her head. "Can't tell you. Not yet."

They started walking again and now Silky was definitely in no mood to talk. Annie's cryptic remark made her frown thoughtfully. Just what did this hard-crusted marshmallow have in mind? Whatever it was, it boded no good for Rex—and probably nothing but trouble for her. Even so, this was her chance to get Rex back. No matter what was flitting around in some dark cranny of her friend's mind, Silky wasn't about to turn back now.

Rex had hurt her, yes. But when Silky had married him, she'd promised that it would be for "better or worse." People go through phases and that's what had happened to Rex. He was over it now, she was sure. Divorce or no, Silky was not ready to call her marriage a failure. She was no quitter. *Failure* was just not a word that she intended to have linked with any area of her life.

She and Rex could—*would*—get back together. After all, she'd changed, too. She'd gone back to get the degree she'd had to abandon when she came to Anchorage as Rex's bride. She'd gotten a good job offer and she looked better, too. At least that's what people had told her since she'd spent so much time biking with freewheeling addict Annie. Surely, Rex would see and appreciate the differences in her. She wasn't just a "little housewife" anymore. All the time they'd been married she'd thought that was what he'd wanted her to be but it hadn't been.

Annie startled her out of her somber reverie with a nudge. "Silk! There's Sag Pack. See? Over there."

Silky looked up in the direction of Annie's excited waving. The shopping mall parking lot was Sunday-morning empty except for fifty-odd bikers organizing for the Anchorage Cyclists' Club's first Annual 'Biked-Alaska,' a trip through the forty-ninth state's vast summer wilderness.

"Where, Annie?" Silky squinted, but couldn't make out anything that looked like *pack*.

"See, over there under the mall sign."

Silky nodded, finally seeing the small fluttering sign that read *Sag*. They increased their pace.

Silky looked around for her ex-husband. Her heart fluttered with nervous anticipation. She didn't see him and hoped that nothing had happened to change his plans. She couldn't imagine going on this extended trip without Rex.

Annie was waving again. "Hi, Beth—Dan. Silky, come on." She called back over her shoulder. "I want you to meet everybody."

Silky pushed to catch up with her animated friend. The bulging panniers over the back wheel of her bike made it much harder to maneuver, something she realized she'd have to quickly get used to. She pulled up into a ragged semicircle of equally burdened bikers—seven of them. No, eight—six males and two females, ranging in ages, Silky guessed, from about fifteen to nearly fifty.

"Silky." Annie touched her arm to get her attention. "I want you to meet our pack leader first. He's fairly new to the club—came from Detroit, I think, but he loves biking." She motioned toward a tall, broad-shouldered man who was busily passing out papers to other members of their group. He was talking quietly. In profile, Silky could see that he was quite attractive. His curly hair shone blue-black in the morning sun, and his features were angular and strong. His lashes were long, dark and curled back, but—turned as he was—she couldn't see the color of his eyes.

He wore a powder blue biker's shirt that had a zippered pocket on the back. His navy shorts were the type made for serious bikers. Especial-

ly constructed for comfort and minimum wind
resistance, they were skin tight. Silky was fasci-
nated by the play of muscles clearly outlined
beneath the stretchy fabric. As he shifted his
weight, the firm hips and broad, corded thighs
flexed, changing the masculine sculpture in
small but extremely intriguing ways. She found
it impossible to look away for fear of missing the
next intimate undulation.

But Annie was insistent. "Silky," she whispered rather sharply for the third time out of the
corner of her mouth. "Here he comes. Try to
stand up straight."

Silky started. "Try to what?"

Annie's face pinkened, and she didn't meet
Silky's eyes. "Uh, nothing." Smiling broadly at
the man coming toward them, she called out,
"Hi, O great leader."

Silky turned back to look at the man. His walk
was graceful—as graceful as any large man
with a slight limp could be expected to be. His
left calf, she could now see, was badly scarred,
no doubt the reason for the slight . . . *limp*?
Scarred!

Her eyes rocketed up to meet his. They were
black—as black as an Alaskan winter's night.
Right now, much to Silky's distress, they sparkled with the same seductive devilment she had
seen over two weeks ago in the hospital. "Oh
no . . ." she moaned, cringing inwardly as he
reached them.

Unaware of Silky's anxiety, Annie held out a
welcoming hand. "Wade, remember I told you

I'd be bringing along a piece of excess baggage? Well"—she extended a sweeping hand toward Silky—"here she is. I want you to meet my roomie, Silky Overbridge."

Silky barely caught Annie's flippant introduction. She was hoping wildly that he wouldn't remember her.

He extended his hand. "We've met." He was smiling at her. "Silky. Short for Silvia Kay. I like it." Taking her hand, he squeezed gently.

Her insides twisted into a tight knot. He hadn't forgotten. Nodding vaguely, she found herself thinking that maybe she should at least be grateful he hadn't said, "Ah, yes, Silvia Kay Overbridge, the hospital nit-wit." "Hello," she said, her voice raspy. She tried swallowing. "How—how's Officer Taylor?"

Wade released her hand slowly. "A little older, a little wiser, but otherwise fine." He handed her a piece of paper from his dwindling stack. "Here's a map of the route and some wilderness safety tips. Glad to have you aboard, Silky." He turned to Annie, who was standing mute. When he handed her a page, she seemed to come awake.

"You—you two have met?" she stammered, not an easy thing to get Annie to do.

Wade slid a quiet glance toward Silky and his grin became teasing and charmingly crooked. She stiffened, waiting. He must have seen her unease, because he answered only, "Yes, briefly, late one night."

Annie's freckles crowded worriedly together

over the bridge of her nose in a confused frown. Before she could pose another question, she was interrupted by a tenor shout.

"Silky!" The voice was as familiar as six years of marriage could make it.

Silky swung her head around to see her ex-husband pedal to a squealing halt inches from her side. Her heart thudded with excited anticipation at their first meeting in so many months.

He looked down at her in that self-assured way he had. His blond hair, straight and closely trimmed, was the same as she remembered, though his forehead seemed a bit higher, the result of a gradually receding hairline. His eyes, the bright blue of an Alaskan summer's sky, were fringed by long, light lashes that were tipped with silver in the sunlight.

Silky inhaled deeply. He was a perfectly beautiful man. Well built, he was more slender than Wade but nearly as tall. As her gaze swept over him, Silky thought how very much like a model he looked now, dressed in striking red biker's shirt and shorts, the shirt sporting a vivid yellow stripe racing diagonally across it. In the stripe, in bold black lettering, were the words *Alaskan Sport*. Looking down the length of his legs, she saw that even his biker's shoes were red and yellow.

"Hi, Sil." One corner of his mouth curved up in a grin that revealed a single slashing dimple. She wordlessly nodded, unable to find her voice as Rex scanned the faces of her two companions. "Oh." His smile faded measurably. "Hello,

Annie. I thought you were riding with Silver Pack."

Annie lifted thin shoulders nonchalantly. "Was, but Silky balked at riding seventy-five miles a day so I decided to ride Sag with her. Sixty miles per is still a pretty good pace."

Rex reached out to shake Wade's hand. He introduced himself. "Rex Overbridge. I manage the 'Alaskan Sport.' We just started carrying biking sports equipment."

Wade withdrew his hand as his dark gaze took inventory of Rex's colorful garb. "Clothes, too, I gather."

Rex nodded. "Definitely. They *do* make the cyclist, don't they?"

Wade's lack of comment spurred Rex on. "I'm taking this little jaunt to advertise the new line—was going to ride with Century Pack, the hundred-milers, but when I found out little Silk was in Sag"—he smiled down at her—"I figured I'd just ride along with you all and help her out."

"Oh? Well, I'm sure Century's loss will be our gain. I'm Wade Banning, Sag Pack leader." He handed Rex a route map. "We'll be getting underway shortly. If you folks will excuse me, I'd better check the others in." He turned toward Silky and Annie, nodding. "Ladies?"

Annie touched his sleeve and said in an overly loud whisper, "You'll learn to love Rex. The man's a prince." Wade's lips quirked with wry humor as he turned away.

Silky shifted a nervous glance to Rex, hoping he hadn't heard. Apparently not. He was busy adjusting the tiny rearview mirror on his safety helmet. She then turned snapping green eyes back toward Annie. The redhead was smiling blandly. Her expression was excruciatingly innocent but her eyes danced as she remarked cheerily, "This trip is going to be fun. I can tell."

Chapter Two

"Hi. Mind if I join you?" Wade asked as he took a seat beside Silky in the shade of a diamond-leaf willow she had chosen, some distance away from the others in the pack.

She looked up, surprised, her half-eaten apple poised at her lips. Lowering it, she smiled tentatively. "Why—uh, no." It wasn't totally the truth. She would have preferred to be eating with either Rex or Annie, but neither one of them seemed to be around just now.

He leaned back against the rough bark. Breaking his Granola bar in half, he offered her a section. "Here. Have some quick energy."

She hesitated. "Oh no. I couldn't take your lunch."

"Sure you could." He laid it in her hand. "I've

already had three." He grinned. "The apple is good, but don't neglect your carbohydrates."

"You sound like my mother."

He laughed out loud. "I like her already." Drawing his knees up, he leaned forward, draping his arms casually about them. "I want you to know I'm glad to have a medically trained person in our pack. I don't anticipate problems, but you never know."

She took a bite of the bar and looked out across the alpine grass. They were by lovely Mirror Lake, twenty-six miles north of Anchorage. She was tired after the morning's ride, but the crisp freshness of the summer breeze ruffling her hair revitalized her and she took a deep breath.

Turning back to him, she was surprised to see how dark and direct his eyes had become. Lowering her lashes, she answered, "I'll be glad to help if I can." She felt a flash of uncomfortable color warm her cheeks at his reminder of their meeting in the hospital. It wasn't a pleasant feeling. With grim determination, she decided that rather than avoid this man for a month, she might as well clear the air once and for all. Swallowing several times before trying her voice again, she finally spoke. "Since you brought it up"—she lifted a shoulder in an apologetic shrug—"I'm really sorry about thinking you were . . . a . . ." She stuttered to a halt as his expression opened in a friendly grin.

"A felon?" he helped. "A crook?"

Her lips quirked into a small smile. She

couldn't help it in the face of his guileless expression. "Yes."

He shook his head. "Don't apologize, Silky. I was working undercover. It was my job to look like a thug." He crunched the last of his Granola bar before running a fist across his clean-shaven jaw. "Worked on that scruffy disguise for two days."

Silky's eyes widened as he went on. "You aren't supposed to tell a cop by his cover, you know. By assuming I was the bad guy, you complimented me."

She was looking down at her hands, now full of apple and Granola bar. A long finger lightly touched her chin, lifting her face to meet dark, soft eyes. "Thanks." His expression was encouraging as he lowered his hand to his bent knee, adding, "Now, you say, 'You're welcome,' and finish that lunch."

His offhand dismissal of something that had been so disconcerting to her put her at ease, and for the first time, she smiled a legitimate smile. "You're welcome." Following orders, she took a bite of her apple and began to relax. She watched the languid sweep of a willow ptarmigan, the Alaskan state bird, as it skimmed the lake for food.

"Say," Wade began conversationally, "how come two people who seem to like each other as much as you and Rex do got divorced?"

The Granola she'd just swallowed became a cloying obstruction in her throat and Silky doubled over in a fit of coughing.

Wade helped with a couple of sharp raps between her shoulderblades. "You okay?"

She waved away his concern. "Ye—yes." She cleared her throat. "How—how did you know about Rex and me?"

He leaned slightly toward her. "Rex Overbridge? *Mrs*. Silvia Kay Overbridge? What kind of a detective would I be if I couldn't figure that out?" After a brief pause, he added with a wide grin, "Besides, Annie told me."

Silky grimaced, her green eyes narrowing. "Figures."

Undaunted, he asked again, "So if you like the guy so much, why the divorce?"

Silky could see that Wade didn't mean to be hurtful. Still, his directness was unsettling. Abruptly, she changed the subject. "I'm glad to see how much your leg has improved since I last saw you. How is this trip going to affect it?"

He chuckled. "You're right. Your divorce is none of my business. Forget it." He straightened the leg in question in front of him. The movement caught Silky's eyes and she watched as he flexed it several times.

"I started riding a stationary bike for therapy after my . . . accident in Detroit. Got hooked on the real thing later. Leading the 'Sag' is therapeutic."

She stretched her legs out too, crossing them at the ankles. With a tired sigh, she said, "Therapy for you, assault and battery for me. My seat must be made of concrete."

She looked up in time to catch his gaze sliding to her hips, clad in white nylon shorts, as he took a slow, careful survey of her softly curving anatomy. A half-smile played across his lips as he remarked, "That wouldn't have been my guess."

Silky's face flushed scarlet at the unexpectedly sensual quality of his deep voice. She swallowed uneasily, but before she could speak, Rex walked swiftly up to them, pushing his bike and sputtering angrily under his breath.

Coming to a stop at their feet, he exploded, "Who the hell is the wise guy?"

Wade frowned, crossing his arms casually over his chest. "Beg pardon?"

Rex gritted through clenched teeth, "Some creep let the air out of my tires when I was—uh, indisposed."

"No!" gasped Silky.

Wade lifted a questioning brow. "Are you sure? Maybe you just had a slow leak."

Rex's light blue eyes flashed angrily. "Am I sure! Of course I'm sure. Just what kind of a fool do you take me for?"

Wade shrugged, rubbing a fist across his mouth and mumbling something that sounded like, "Not sure yet." Or did he? Silky couldn't be absolutely certain.

Rex blurted, "Well! What are you going to do about this?"

Wade shrugged wide shoulders and slowly stood up, dusting off his shorts as he straightened. Nodding at Rex, he turned toward the main gathering. "Say!" he called loudly, "Did anyone let the air out of this man's tires?"

The bikers, lounging in small groups or standing idly beside their bikes, all stared blankly back or shook their heads in the negative.

Silky saw Annie now, seated cross-legged beside a young married couple, Beth and Dan. Annie's expression was every bit as bewildered as the others'.

Wade nodded, apparently satisfied. "Okay, thanks." Turning back to Rex, he said, "Well, Overbridge, it looks like you just ran into some prankster passing by. Next time, you might take your bike into the woods with you."

Rex's look was one of complete astonishment. "What? You mean to tell me that's all you're going to do about this?"

Wade pursed his lips in thought. "Can't really do much, Rex. I didn't have room on the bike for my lie detector, so I guess we'll just have to take these folks' word for it this time."

"And that's it! That's all? I had to walk this thing six miles, you realize."

"Six miles," Wade repeated, shaking his head and looking concerned, but not overly so. "You don't have a pump, I take it."

Rex snarled back, "If I did, I wouldn't have had to walk!"

"Too bad." Wade took hold of the handle bars. "Well, I do. Have your lunch and get some rest while I pump this up. We'll be leaving in about ten minutes." With a friendly nod toward Silky, Wade led the bike away.

Silky stood and stretched, brushing the crumbs of her dehydrated dinner from her lap. It was after ten o'clock, but still dusky light on this long, Alaskan summer evening. Dinner over, most of the pack were either quietly talking around the dwindling embers of the camp's fire, or pitching their one-man tents.

Silky was bone weary but, after spending most of the last year working nights, she found it hard to imagine going to bed this early. Besides, she felt grimy. She wondered if she really could hear the faint gurgle of a stream from the nearby woods.

She decided it wouldn't hurt to check. Pulling a robe, soap and a towel from her pannier, she walked off into the Alaskan twilight along a woodland path.

Yes. The gurgling grew louder. Silky smiled when she finally saw the water sparkling beyond the trees. Reaching the grassy shore, she looked around. Deciding that she was safely alone, she stripped off her white tank top and shorts, shoes and socks, leaving on only her brief bra and panties.

Just as she moved to unfasten the catch between her breasts, a hand slid boldly around to her bare stomach. "You've lost a little weight," a familiar voice whispered near her ear. "I might add, you're looking great." His fingers pulled her back, kneading the skin lightly.

She sucked in a surprised breath. "Rex! W—what are you doing here?"

He turned her to him. His smile was dashing, making her knees quiver. He laughed brightly, pulling her close. "What do you think I'm doing? I'm getting off alone in the woods with my favorite lady." One hand slid down her back to cup a rounded hip, and he moaned into her throat, "Oh, Sil, you feel so good." He pulled her against the long, lean frame she remembered so well. She was made very aware of his aroused state and she found herself stiffening at the realization. Rather than being pleased that Rex wanted her, she felt an odd, angry knot form in her throat and a queer surge of hurt sting her eyes. How dare he come here and take her into his arms again like this as though nothing had changed between them, as though the past year of pain and loneliness had never existed!

He'd noticed that she'd lost weight. Yes, she certainly had. For the first two months after he'd walked out, she hadn't been able to eat or sleep. If it hadn't been for Annie's constantly shoveling food into her and insisting that she get out into the fresh air on all those maniacal bicycle rides —if it hadn't been for Annie's constant nagging that finally convinced Silky to enroll at the university—well, she just didn't know where she'd be now. Now. She sucked her lips nervously between her teeth.

What was she going to do? This wasn't how she'd pictured their reconciliation at all. She'd expected an apology, a little wooing, not to be fondled as though he'd only been away on an extended business trip.

"Rex." She pressed her hands against his red-and-yellow-clad chest. "Please." She pushed hard, and he lifted his head.

"Please what, darling?" His voice was heavy with desire.

She watched him tentatively through her lashes. Never in her wildest imaginings had she thought that she'd be put in the position of fending off the very man she wanted back! But this way was no good, somehow. It wasn't right.

She reached behind her back and pulled his hand away from its intimate hold on her. "I—I." She paused, unsure of what to say. She didn't want to anger him but she needed more time. They both needed more time. Lowering her gaze, she decided to take the easy route. "Somebody might see us."

His face clouded. "But, honey, it's been such a long time." He would have taken her into his arms again but she stepped out of his reach.

"Yes, yes it has." Her jaw worked with the devastating memory of how long and miserable a time it had been. "Please go back to camp, Rex."

He dragged a hand through his hair and exhaled heavily. "Well, maybe you're right." He nodded gravely. "I'll go on back."

She felt an odd combination of relief and sadness wash over her. "Yes, I think that would be best."

He reached out and tugged at one of her

pigtails. His half-smile was vaguely teasing. "Later, then, pretty lady."

He turned away and walked back along the path, his every step deflating Silky in a way she couldn't fathom. Her eyes filled with ridiculous tears as she finished undressing. Why? Why was she sad? She sniffed, wiping at her damp cheek as she dropped her underthings on the grass and listlessly waded into the water. It was frigid, but she hardly felt it. She was numb.

Her dreams and fantasies of her first intimate reunion with Rex had been so—so different from this scene in the woods. It was true, he'd come to her, and he obviously wanted her. But he hadn't apologized or fallen to his knees begging her forgiveness, agonizing about how he'd been very, very wrong and that he knew now that she was the only woman in the world for him. That's what she'd thought—hoped—he'd do.

As she soaped herself, she tried to shake off her depression. After all, hadn't he proved he did want her back? That was a start.

A few minutes later she toweled herself, feeling clean, refreshed and bolstered by a new hope in her heart. Rex would come around. She just knew he would. He had to!

Slipping on her short, mauve terry robe, she scooped up her discarded clothing. Tomorrow would be another day. There was plenty of time.

"Ready?"

Silky was so startled by the disembodied voice that had apparently been posed by one of the more inquisitive trees that she dropped her bundle of clothes, gasping, *"What?"*

Before she could recover, Wade Banning stepped out from behind a spruce. He ignored her question as he gathered up her spilled underthings and wrapped them in the towel with her other clothes. Handing the bundle back to her, he said, "I asked if you were ready to go back?"

He must have been out there watching her for some time, Silky realized with horrible certainty. Her face began to burn with indignant rage. "Just—just how long have you been spying on me?"

He smiled crookedly. "Not spying. Guarding."

"Guarding?" she rasped, clutching her clothes like a shield. "Guarding what?"

"You, of course." He cocked his dark head to indicate the path. "These north woods trails aren't made by people, you know. They're made by moose and bear."

Her anger had grown so intense that her mouth worked soundlessly for a moment before she could find her voice. "Oh, sure! You expect me to believe that you were worried that I'd be attacked by a wandering moose! No, Mr. Banning. I'm not swallowing that. You were sneaking around in the trees watching me take a bath!" Her voice was quivery and high-pitched.

He took a step forward and faced her squarely. There was mild curiosity in his expression. "Do you really believe I get my kicks sneaking peeks at women through the bushes?" When he said it that way, a man as attractive and agressive as he clearly was, the suggestion did seem rather ludicrous.

"Do you?" He raised a sardonic brow.

She hedged. "Well . . . if you weren't—uh, doing that, then *you* explain why you were lurking in the trees."

Gazing down at her with the most infuriating amusement, he said, "I was writing."

She lifted her chin regally. "I don't believe you."

"Fine," he said, lifting his arms as though under arrest. "Search me."

"Writing? Guarding? Maybe you'd better get your story straight, Lieutenant," Silky snapped.

Wade pulled a small notebook from the pocket in the back of his shirt. "I was making an entry in the trip log. I like to find a quiet spot to gather my thoughts." He flipped it open to a page marked "June 16, Day one." The page was filled with a strong, masculine scrawl. Silky's chin lost some of its imperial angle as he continued, "I didn't realize you were even out here until I heard you and Rex . . . talking."

The pause in his explanation let her know that he was well aware of what had gone on between them, and she felt herself go crimson with renewed anger and embarrassment. "Well—why didn't you make yourself known? Apparently you're no gentleman!"

"You're probably right," he said straightforwardly as he put the notebook back into his shirt. A wry smile lifted one corner of his mouth when his dark eyes settled on hers again. "But it's always been my policy never to interfere with a happily divorced couple. Besides, you looked like you were handling the situation pretty well all by yourself."

"*Looked!*" She jammed her hands on her hips, totally disregarding the fact that frilly things scattered all around their path. "Then you did look, admit it!"

He prudently kept his face straight, but Silky's insides churned to see the unrepentant laughter in his eyes. "Yes, for a minute. But as soon as I realized you were only half-dressed, I closed one eye." His wide shoulders dropped as he bent once again to get her clothes. This time he didn't hand them back but held the bundle clutched in one big fist. He took her elbow. "Maybe we'd better get back—bears, remember?"

She jerked out of his grip. "I think I'd rather take my chances with them, if you don't mind."

"Oh, but I do. It'd be a real blot on my record if I lost somebody the first night out." He took her elbow again, this time firmly enough to draw her to an abrupt halt.

She turned, planning to toss a cutting remark, but instead of meeting his eyes, she found her lips disconcertingly near his ear. He'd leaned down so close that his warm breath tickled the base of her throat.

Silky had no idea how to react. There wasn't anything threatening in his action, nor was there anything sexually aggressive about it. He was merely leaning . . . and sniffing? "What do you think you're doing?"

She could feel the soft exhale of his laugh against her skin. The feathery touch of his lips on her throat was tantalizing as he murmured, "You smell like a field of lilies of the valley." She felt bereft of his warmth when he lifted his head. "You're going to have to get rid of that perfumed soap. Bears are attracted to it."

Bears are attracted to it! A crazy sense of disappointment seized her as he began to walk, pulling her along. Gritting her teeth, she frowned, thinking peevishly, *Bears, maybe, but certainly not police lieutenants.* Lifting a hand, she pushed a branch out of her way. What did it matter to her what his taste in fragrance was, anyway? A bit more irritably than she had intended, she muttered, "I think I'd notice a bear before it got *that* close."

He laughed delightedly. "Their ability to catch scents is much keener than ours. Trust me. I'll lend you a bar of my soap. It's unscented."

He helped her pick her way across a fallen log as she quipped, "I'm forever in your debt."

His grin was easy. "There's good news." Releasing her arm, he walked silently beside her as Silky's pique simmered just below a boil. This path hadn't seemed nearly so long on her walk in.

Wade broke the tense silence after a moment. "Are you going to take him back?"

Involuntarily she caught her breath, shocked at the outlandishly personal question. *"What!"*

"I asked—"

"I heard what you *asked*. I just can't believe you asked it!" She heaved a sigh that could have been an obscenity, it was so full of overtones.

He touched her back to prod her forward again. She hadn't realized she'd stumbled to a halt. He went on conversationally. "Whatever it was that made you throw him out—"

She blurted out, "I didn't throw him out, he left me—" She snapped her mouth shut in horror. How could she have allowed herself to say that, and to a virtual stranger, too! She writhed inside.

He immediately pulled her to face him. His own features were open and incredulous, and Silky was surprised to see that his dark eyes were black with anger. "You? The man left *you?*" His hands were squeezing her shoulders, and she winced. Mortified, she turned her face away. His voice was low and subdued. "Silky. Why?"

She worked hard at collecting herself enough to speak. She whispered raggedly, "Let go of me. My personal life is none of your business." She reached up with trembling fingers and jerked his hands away.

Pivoting, she started to run, but he was ready for her flight, catching her hand in his. "Mind if I try something?" he asked quietly.

It was a rhetorical question. Before she could

voice any objections his mouth molded itself gently to hers. A large hand moved possessively around her. His fingers opened, spreading over her lower back as he pulled her against him. His hand moved slowly, deliberately, caressing and relaxing the stiffened spine until she was arched deeply into his broad, muscular frame.

His lips were pliant, instructive, teaching her things about this unpredictable man that she'd never intended to know. His tongue spoke eloquently as it teased and tempted her lips. The intimacy of the touch was a primer, a first lesson, inspiring a warming desire in Silky to know what was yet to come. She found herself opening her lips wider, against her will and better judgment.

Her breathing became erratic, and her heartbeat was soon affected in the same absurd way as his tongue slid deeper into the inviting recesses of her mouth. She sighed weakly, like a baby bird suddenly needing the life-giving nourishment his kiss was offering. Wade was affecting her in a physical way that went far beyond her most uncontrolled moments with Rex.

Her arms slid slowly up the front of his body-hugging shirt to capture his neck. She moved one hand up to tangle shaking fingers in the springy black curls, and to press his kiss even more deeply into hers.

Silky moaned deep in her throat, enjoying the melting sensations he was setting free within her, enjoying too the sweet, damp earthiness of the pungent pines as the natural scents of the forest mingled with Wade's musky maleness. With thoughtless abandon, she pressed her thinly covered breasts even more intimately against his hard chest. As she did, she could feel the bass-drum pounding of his heart increase its tempo against her stimulated nipples.

With the sensual movement of her body, he groaned against her lips, finally, with great reluctance, lifting his mouth from hers. He murmured unevenly, "You kiss—like you do it for a living, Silky." Light, nibbling lips teased her cheek and made her quiver within his arms as he went on, "Did he leave you because you were seeing other men?"

The whispered question hit her like an avalanche. "That's insulting!" she cried hoarsely.

Wade's dark eyes drew her into a tangled web of confusing emotions. His expression was serious as he murmured, "I'd hoped it would be."

Though she struggled to be free of his imprisoning arms, he wouldn't release her. If he had, she knew she probably would have fallen to the ground. There was no strength left in her rubbery legs.

With the tenacity of a bloodhound, he went relentlessly on, his voice low and slightly strained. "Rex was seeing someone on the side, then." Black brows lifted. "You have to give the guy credit for his brass, following you out there like that after what he did to you." Wade shook his head at the thought. "You were nicer than most women in your position would have been."

Silky bristled. "My position?" So! He thought

he knew so much about everything! She decided to throw a monkey wrench in the works and dent that "Wade Banning, most-clever detective" suit of armor he wore so proudly! She snapped, "You're wrong about my position, Lieutenant Banning. Did it ever occur to you that people change? People *can* make mistakes and learn from them, you know." Exasperated, she yelled, "Just so there won't be any doubt in your mind, I am planning that Rex and I . . ." Her words dwindled away as she watched his lips curl into a crooked grimace. She was surprised to see a muscle begin to flex tensely in his jaw.

"You're planning that Rex and you what? Learn to tolerate each other? Come to some agreement on who gets Aunt Martha's antique lamp? What?" The questions were bitten out between his clenched teeth.

Struggling to control herself, Silky knitted shaky fingers together, eyeing him unflinchingly. "Isn't there some rule that you have to read me my rights *before* you start grilling, Lieutenant?" She grabbed her bundle of clothes from his hand and attempted to turn away, but he caught her arm.

"Hell, woman! You don't mean *you* want him back?"

She jerked out of his hold and turned back to face him. Her lips trembled, and her voice was distressingly unsteady. "That's none of your business!"

"My God, Silky!" he breathed. "The man's not worth—" The slap that stung his face was fueled by months of smoldering frustration and defeat —months of listening to Annie's heated diatribes —months of defending her position, her feelings. Now all those pent-up emotions were kindled into an explosive rage by Wade's unfair judgment. He didn't know Rex. He didn't know her. He had no right to criticize her decisions one way or the other. No one did! She could make it with Rex, and it was no one's affair if she wanted him back.

Wade's disbelieving face blurred as her stormy eyes filled with tears. "You know where you can go with your opinions!" she suggested in a desperately controlled voice.

A wan smile twisted his lips, and he rubbed his reddened cheek. "Nice going, Banning," he mumbled disgustedly to no one in particular. Silky had spun away, fleeing his unwelcome, unsettling presence.

Chapter Three

 h—what?" Silky blinked moss green eyes, realizing with a small jolt that she had been watching Wade's romanesque profile and had completely missed what Rex had just said. He repeated, with a tolerant chuckle, "I asked if you're ready. Where were you just then?"

She smiled a bit weakly and fibbed, "I was just looking at the dew sparkling on the grass and leaves." It didn't matter that she'd really been looking at Wade. It was a small, unimportant lie. She continued, "You know, Rex, I never imagined how crisp and beautiful mornings out here could be."

"They're nice. But you're the most beautiful thing out here, in my opinion." He grinned down at her; the bright morning sun was doing exciting, golden things to his hair.

Silky inhaled happily at the compliment. *That* was more like it. Rex was beginning to act like the man she'd fallen in love with. The smile that lifted her lips was now genuine, and she felt positive that today was going to be a magnificent one!

Rex dropped a casual arm about her shoulders. "Grab your bike, Sil. It looks like everybody is about packed up and ready to go." He lightly propelled her toward the group that was gathering on the gravel drive that circled in front of the log youth hostel—and toward Wade.

It wasn't a direction she preferred, but she was with Rex, so she relaxed a little. For the past five days, since her unexpectedly disturbing encounter with Wade, she had single-mindedly avoided him. And, as for venturing out alone in the woods again, she hadn't needed to. So far. They'd camped outside youth hostels that had provided bath houses.

As a matter of fact, the only contact she'd had with Wade since that first day had been when he'd surprised her outside of the women's bathhouse, and handed her a bar of soap. She recalled vividly how one corner of his mouth had lifted in what seemed like an apologetic smile as he'd said, "It's unscented." Then he'd turned away, leaving her no time to respond, or to give the soap back, which had been her immediate inclination. So, she'd taken the soap and used it. If it had been anything else, she wouldn't have kept it; but pride was one thing, and stupidity another entirely! After all, who needs bears?

Besides, she reasoned, didn't Wade *owe* her an apology for his uncalled-for remarks? Maybe this bar of soap was the apology. Next, Wade might even offer to wash his own mouth out with it!

Silky's eyes flicked back up. There he was again! Lately, he always seemed to be directly blocking her line of vision. He was talking quietly with Annie and a small man named Leonard, an Anchorage librarian. Yesterday, Leonard had sat down with them at lunch, talking more to Annie than to anyone, as he explained that he was new to the bicycling club, and was taking this trip to get to know people. It was obvious that he wanted to get to know Annie, especially.

Silky's expression held a touch of sadness as she looked at him. With his slight build, vulnerable gray eyes and incongruous but endearing walrus moustache, he looked a little fragile for the job he was taking on.

Good luck, Leonard, Silky thought, doubting that he had much of a chance. Annie turned men into enemies with almost more devotion than she turned walk-in browsers at her dealership into Jeep owners! Well, she sighed inwardly, maybe Annie would go a little easier on this one.

Her eyes shifted from Leonard to Wade, who was over a head taller and nearly twice as broad. His black eyes were on her—again, as they had been for more times than she cared to remember these past five days. His look was steady and direct as always, and she almost felt as though he were watching her for some sign of forgiveness.

He smiled as they walked by. It was friendly, almost hopeful. "Morning, folks."

She nodded curtly and looked away without returning the smile. Rex answered for them. "Looks like it'll be another nice day."

Wade sounded a little doubtful. "Seems chilly, to me."

Silky knew that his remark was directed at her, but she didn't care. She'd had enough of his opinions the first day out.

"What the—" Rex's arm dropped from Silky's shoulder and he hurried ahead. She watched him sprint toward his bike, where a boy was crouched beside the back wheel, his back toward them. Silky recognized the youngster as the pack's youngest member, thirteen-year-old Randy Douglas. She couldn't see what he was doing, but apparently Rex felt he was up to no good. He was shouting, "Hey, kid, what do you think you're doing there!"

The boy turned, screwing his face up in a sunburned squint. "Huh?"

Silky walked up beside Rex as he demanded again, "I said, *what* are you doing? That equipment is very expensive!"

"Yeah? How much did it cost?"

Rex snorted. "That's none of your business."

Randy shrugged disinterestedly and stood. "Okay, mister. You brought it up, not me." Silky pursed her lips to keep from smiling at the youth's deadpan wit.

Rex scowled down at him. "Don't you be smart with me, son."

"I ain't your son, man!" Randy shot back, his brown eyes flashing angrily.

Silky felt an unexpected pang of sympathy for the boy. "Rex, I—I'm sure Randy didn't mean any harm." She turned encouraging eyes to the youth. "Did you?"

"Naw. I was just lookin'."

"Well—" Rex expelled the word in an exasperated sigh. Silky could tell he was trying to soften his manner, and she admired him for the attempt. He'd never been fond of children, but he was trying. "I guess looking is all right, but you ask me first, next time. Okay?"

"Yeah, sure," Randy answered without enthusiasm as he swatted a mosquito on his arm.

Silky didn't know much about kids, but Randy had seemed sullen and solitary the whole trip so far. She could see that he was very unhappy about something. So was his father, if a gloomy expression and slumped shoulders could tell anything. There was trouble between them, though she didn't know what. Whatever it might be, it was a sad thing to see reflected in those guarded, young eyes.

She held out a hand, trying for friendship. "Randy, I don't think we've been properly introduced. I'm Silky Overbridge."

He shrugged again, shoving his fists into the pockets of his ragged cut-off jeans and dropping his gaze to his scuffed tennis shoes. "Big deal."

Feeling embarrassed and a little irritated by his unexpected rejection, she let her hand drop to her side, unsure of what to do next.

"Look, boy!" Rex's voice had taken on an edge. "You watch how you talk to the lady or I won't show you the bike."

Randy curled his thin upper lip in distaste. "Who cares. Those Italian bikes are for fairies, anyway."

"Fairies!" The muscles in Rex's neck tensed. "Listen, kid. Just don't let me catch you messing around with my bike ever again."

Randy lifted his blunt chin defiantly, his expression an unpleasant mixture of disgust and disinterest. "Don't worry, mister. You won't." His sullen eyes shifted to Silky and held on her face for a moment before he turned away and trudged off.

"Juvenile delinquent!" There was scorn in Rex's terse accusation. "You try being nice to the kid and see what it gets you? Insults!"

Silky looked up at him. "I don't know, Rex. He looks like he's got troubles."

"He *is* trouble, if you ask me! Kids like that belong in a detention home."

"Have you ever been inside one?" Wade's quiet question came from behind her, and Silky cocked her head around to look at him. He was very near, resting his hand lightly on her racing saddle.

Rex frowned at the unexpected challenge. "Of course not, but—"

Wade lifted a sardonic brow. "If you had, Overbridge, you wouldn't say that." He moved up to face them. "Sorry, didn't mean to eavesdrop. I just wanted to tell you that since it's pretty windy, we'll be riding in a tight pack."

In keeping with her policy to avoid Wade, Silky turned toward Rex, asking, "What's a tight pack? Do I dare hope it's an air-conditioned bus?"

Rex smiled indulgently, his irritation melting away. "No, sweetheart. It's when bikers get as close together as possible. Actually, it's called *drafting*. The lead rider bucks the wind resistance so that everybody following has it easier. The closer you can get to the bike in front of you, the better it works."

Silky was worried. "Just how close do you have to get? Six, seven feet I hope?"

Rex laughed and pulled her safety helmet from the handlebars of her bike, fitting it carefully on her head. "No, you little goose," he teased. "It's more like an inch."

Horrified at the thought of speeding along a highway in the middle of an easily unbalanced bicycle sandwich, Silky squeaked, *"An inch!"* She shook her head firmly. "No thanks! An inch is how you measure slacks' hems and low-heeled shoes, not the distance between two-wheeled instruments of destruction. I'll just lag my usual half-mile behind and do my own bucking! I'd rather have wind in my teeth than spokes!"

Wade crossed his arms loosely over his chest, smiling at her vigorous rejection. She thought she could detect a touch of sympathy in his eyes. "Don't worry, Silky. Since we're not competitive racers, six or eight inches will be fine. It won't be as bad as you think."

Her expression was skeptical. "The last time I heard *that*, I was about to have four wisdom teeth pulled."

Rex let out a laugh, smoothing her hair as it danced freely in a gust of wind. "I'll never forget that. There were complications." He turned toward Wade, explaining, "After four days, Silky's mouth was still packed. She couldn't eat. She couldn't talk. She was miserable. Every time she saw her oral surgeon, she'd mumble curses at him."

Silky slid a glance toward Wade. His expression was bland as he listened.

"Finally," Rex was continuing, "just before she left the hospital—almost a week later than planned—her doctor told her that he'd understood every unladylike thing she'd said!"

Silky blushed behind already sun-pinkened cheeks. "I gather they take a course in mumbling. That's how they can carry on perfectly normal two-sided conversations with people when they've got three fingers, cotton, a mirror and a drill in their patient's mouth."

Wade made a noncommittal grunt. His expression was still pleasant, but there was less warmth in it now. Apparently he hadn't been completely taken with their trek down memory lane. Indicating the others in their group with a nod, he said, "I think we'd better be going."

He'd taken a couple of uneven steps away when Silky noticed that he was limping a little more than he had the day before. Despite her vow to ignore him, she couldn't help but call out, "Wade—" She stammered to a stop as he turned toward her, lifting a questioning brow.

He was surprised that she'd spoken directly to him. "Yes?"

Swallowing, she suggested quietly, "Uh . . . try not to overwork that leg."

He flashed her a grateful smile. "Thanks." As he turned away, he called out with a surprising amount of enthusiasm, "Okay, folks. Let's saddle up. Today we make Fairbanks!"

As she swung her leg across her bike, Silky wondered at herself. Why had she said that, when she'd promised herself to flatly ignore the man? She grimaced, recalling the sparkle in his dark eyes as he'd thanked her for her concern. He had known at that moment that he'd been forgiven—almost before she had realized it. Damn him for his infuriating intuitiveness, anyway. But, then, there was just something about him that wouldn't allow her to stay angry with him for long—not really angry. Bothered, yes. Troubled, a little. But not angry. He was so doggedly insistent on being friendly and helpful it was impossible to dislike him.

Oh well. She sighed. Maybe she just wasn't

cut out to carry a grudge. Besides, they were going to be together for several weeks yet. It would be best this way.

"You go on ahead of me, Sil. I'll bring up the rear," Rex directed as they began to form up in the tight pack with Wade in the lead position.

Silky nodded as she moved in behind Annie. She called up to her friend. "Look, Evel Knievel Toone, I know you love to live on the razor's edge of disaster, but try not to make any sudden detours. I don't want to have your handlebars for lunch."

Annie's laugh was derisive. "Listen, kid. I've got a crazy librarian in front of me who just admitted he has a depth-perception problem, so don't pester me with your little troubles."

Silky groaned miserably. "You're a big help."

They'd been riding for a little less than two hours, crouched against heavy head winds, when the news was passed back that they could finally see the mighty Mount McKinley, also known as Denali, standing sentinel over its vast, six-million-acre national park.

Silky had grown relatively comfortable with the moderate pace and, surprisingly, she also felt fairly good about her six-inch distance from Annie's back wheel. At least she was secure enough in her ability by now to look up at the distant mountain.

The billowy clouds that had masked its face from view for three days had finally parted, revealing the huge block of granite in all its craggy beauty.

"It's the tallest mountain on earth," shouted Annie, passing along Leonard's information. "And Denali is a wildlife preserve. Leonard says we might see a grizzly—maybe even wolves along the road."

"Shut up, Annie!" Silky shot back sharply as an eighteen-wheeler thundered by. She leaned hard away from the sucking action that pulled her bike toward the highway. The grade was a long uphill grind, and Silky was panting heavily. Her nerves were frayed by the combined effects of crouching against the wind and the heavy currents created by the big semis that traveled the busy George Parks Highway. She felt so pushed and pulled by all the natural—and unnatural—buffeting, she thought she'd collapse if she didn't rest soon.

She could see Wade point emphatically down to the left. Pressing her lips together, she renewed her concentration. That was the signal for a hazard ahead. What was it this time? A hole? Broken glass? She steeled herself, once again, for disaster. Pedaling hard, she dodged the hazard in her turn. It was a broken beer bottle. She shook her head at the thoughtlessness of some people. To clutter this beautiful, virgin country was, to Silky, an unforgivable crime.

Once the immediate threat of upending in broken glass was past, she felt fatigue grip her again. Was she the *only* one in the pack who was on the verge of collapse? She slumped, crouching lower and watching Annie's back wheel carefully. Wade's pace was slower than normal, and she was grateful. At this point, it was the only thing that was keeping her going. How was Wade managing, bearing the brunt of this? He must be half-dead by now.

She flicked her eyes to her watch, sighing tiredly. It was only ten-thirty. There would be at least another hour before they stopped for lunch. Gritting her teeth with stubborn resolve and wincing at the sandy feeling in her mouth, she bent her head and pushed into the wind.

"Damn it! This is ridiculous!"

At first Silky was startled by the unexpected sound, wondering how her thoughts had taken a masculine voice. But then she became aware that Rex had pedaled up beside her. "Sil, I'm going on up ahead. Obviously Wade's getting tired." He began to pull on ahead as he finished, "At this rate, we'll never make Fairbanks tonight."

Before Silky could puff out her opinion that Wade's "obviously tired" pace was about as grueling as she could stand, Rex was gone. She should have realized that she wasn't in good enough condition to be on this trip! Just because she was dying, didn't mean that everyone else was. If Rex had his way, it looked like it would get worse before it got better.

She was pulled sharply out of her morose

thoughts by Annie's yell. *"Hey, Rex!* Get out of the road! Those truckers aren't going to like you slowing them down!"

Rex ignored her words and pushed on up toward the front of the pack. Annie glanced over her shoulder, beyond Silky, who was now last in line. As Silky watched, Annie's expression changed from irritated to horrified. An instant later, Silky knew why. She could hear a truck approaching loudly, its gears grinding in an effort to slow its massive forward movement.

"Oh hell!" Annie moaned.

Silky stiffened with alarm, choking out, "Annie, tell Rex!"

Annie jerked her head back to see Rex pedaling up the middle of the right lane. She screamed at the top of her lungs, "Rex, you idiot! Get out of the way!"

Silky paled, her palms going slick with sweat. "Please, Rex—please move!" She squeaked out the plea.

A blow, a physical concussion of sound, boomed into Silky's ears. It happened again in several quick blasts as the furious trucker pounded on his mighty air horn.

"God!" Silky gasped, her heart in her throat. Thank heaven she was last in line. If anyone had been behind her, he would have rammed into her bike when her legs froze in panic. But her recovery was rapid enough to avoid either a bad spill or even a complete stop—and it was just in time for her to cower as the frustrated

trucker, unable to pass on the hill, down shifted again. Silky strained forward to look for Rex, and was relieved to see that he'd finally gotten out of the way.

Silky pulled over, having had just about enough emotional and physical trauma for the moment. Without thinking, she glanced up at the truck's cab as it passed, and shuddered at the enraged face of the driver. He shook his fist at the bikers as his semi crawled past them up the long grade. Silky wasn't sure that the man in the truck was pleased at missing Rex.

Annie hopped from her bike and waved broadly, shouting out a cheery, "Peace and love to you, too, brother!" Pulling off her safety helmet, she ran a shaky hand through damp curls. "Whew! I have a feeling that guy wasn't inviting us to lunch." She turned toward Silky as she put her helmet back on her head. "You okay, kiddo?"

Silky's heart was thudding wildly and her legs were trembling with fatigue. "I—I thought Rex was . . ."—her lips trembled with the memory— "going to be killed!"

Annie flicked down her kickstand with an annoyed swing of her foot. "Should have been, the fool! When somebody pulls a stupid stunt like Rex did, it's just like stealing to those drivers. They lose momentum, time and money. I don't blame the guy for being mad."

Silky bristled defensively. "Rex was just concerned about Wade being tired."

"Well, he could have contained his concern for

two more minutes, Silky. He—" Annie stopped short, compressing her lips together in a thin line. Maybe Silky's distress at having Rex criticized had showed in her expression. She didn't know. But she was grateful that Annie had decided not to pursue the argument. Annie exhaled heavily. "I'll shut up, Silky. No sense beating you to death with it."

Both Silky and Annie turned to notice for the first time that their entire group had stopped. Many were taking advantage of the unexpected break with a cool squirt from their water bottles, some over their heads, some into their mouths. A drink seemed like an excellent idea to Silky. She pulled her bottle from its case and straightened. As she drank, she watched Wade walking his bike slowly along the edge of the gravel shoulder that bordered a field of erratically nodding wild flowers. He smiled when his eyes caught hers, and she found it hard to swallow her sip of water.

Annie called out to him. "Hi, chief. To what do we owe this honor?"

He pulled up beside her, answering, "Rex offered to spell me for a while."

Annie's laugh was derisive. "Oh? So that's what he was doing. I thought he was trying out for the Olympic Stupidity team!"

Wade grinned. "Well—" He slid a quick, appraising glance toward Silky before continuing, "Whatever—I can sure use the break. That wind is fierce."

Silky had tensed with Annie's caustic remark. But Wade's quiet, uncritical answer drained away her urge to pounce. Instead, she smiled and said, "Welcome to the caboose." She started to pull her bike back a little to make room for him in front of her. "Here, you ride behind Annie."

"No, thanks." Wade had moved quickly, dropping a halting hand on her handlebar. "I'll follow you."

"But you'll be eating everybody's dirt," she objected, without much basis in logic. After all, that's just what she'd been doing. But, something in her was disturbed by the idea of having him watch her.

He flashed her an easy smile. "I can eat a little dirt—and a few words. If I dish it out, I guess I should be able to take it."

Silky's mouth dropped open. He wasn't talking about dirt, or even riding, anymore. He was actually apologizing! She stared wordlessly at him. It was really quite ironic, somehow. Here she was, waiting with bated breath for some show of apology from Rex, and out of the blue, she got one from Wade—and for something so much less important!

She felt his hand touch hers before it closed around her wrist. "Look, Silky, about the other night—" Lowering his head so that Annie couldn't hear, he murmured, "I'm really sorry." She was caught by the earnest expression on his face and felt the circle of warm strength his fingers made about her arm as he added, almost too softly for her to hear, "You were right. It wasn't—isn't my business."

She swallowed, her green eyes lost somewhere deep in the black endlessness of his. For what seemed like a long time, she could only study his face, unable to form an answer. At last, she found herself nodding. "Forget it, Wade." It came out in a whisper. "Let's just forget it."

A slight smile touched his lips, but before he could respond, Annie spoke. "Uh, oh."

They turned toward her as she inclined her head to indicate something going on ahead. "It looks like we're being signaled to start."

Silky groaned, her mind lurching back to reality. "Already?" She suggested wearily, "Look, you all go on. I've just got to rest a while, but I promise I'll be along shortly." That was a lie. She didn't know if she'd ever be "along" again. Her legs quivered with overexertion. All her muscles wanted was an immediate release from the responsibility of supporting her, of propelling her forward—for a good, long while.

Annie frowned. "Honey, we can't just leave—"

Wade touched Annie's arm, halting her objection. "I'll stay with her. You, my expert, can bring up the rear for a while."

Annie's lips curled into a satisfied smirk as she squinted up at him. "Now there's an idea. Why didn't I think of it!"

Leonard's tenor voice interrupted them as he

called back over his shoulder, "Hey, Toone, you ready?"

Annie crinkled her freckled nose in distaste and shot back a pithy rebuff, "Not for you, little man!" She waved him off with a quick flick of her hand. "Get along, you librarian."

Leonard's high-pitched laugh was quick and real as Annie swung onto her bike and was off, inches behind the chuckling man's narrow rear wheel.

"Oh, *no!*" Silky sputtered, pulling her arm from his light hold. "Wade, please. You go on. I'll be all right. I—I just need a few minutes to get my—uh—"

He was shaking his head in a way that made Silky very sure that her protests were falling on deaf ears. He took her water bottle and bent to snap it back into its holder. "There's this rule, Silky, that says a pack leader can't leave tired bikers alone on wilderness highways. After a while it tends to clutter the natural setting." Straightening, he cocked his head toward the flower-filled meadow. "Let's move away from the road. There's a nice crop of willows over there."

She watched the others disappear over the hill and wondered at the panic she felt. "On second thought, Wade, I think I'm ready to go on."

He had turned away toward the field, but at her objection he turned back, peering narrowly down at her. Shaking his head, he said, "Look, Silky. I thought I'd apologized for the other night. If I promise to be on my best behavior, will you rest for five minutes?"

A furious flush of embarrassment rushed up her neck, pinkening her face. "Oh—don't be silly, Wade." Her voice sounded oddly shrill. What was wrong with her? Certainly she knew Wade would be nothing less than a gentleman. What exactly was her problem? She had forgiven him, but for some reason she wasn't ready to spend time alone with him—not yet. "Wade, I—I hate to be—uh, responsible for taking you away from the pack. Honestly, I'm fine." She worked hard to make her smile look bright and energetic.

When he didn't answer right away, she reluctantly lifted her eyes to meet his. He was watching her intently, and she thought she saw something like laughter quirk one corner of his mouth. He challenged casually, "I dare you to look me straight in the chin and say that." His shrug was unconcerned. "Besides, the only person responsible for what I do is me." He touched her hand as it lay draped loosely on a curving handlegrip. "Come on."

Without waiting for her to reply, he turned away, his wide shoulders swinging around with a confident grace. He seemed to know she wouldn't make any further objections. She knew it too. She was very tired, and she wasn't stupid enough to stand there and deny that fact any longer. She pushed her bike into the tall grass, following him toward a small stand of swaying willows some distance from the highway.

After taking a seat in the shade, she busied nervous fingers smoothing her pink tank top down over matching shorts. Trying to appear calm, she leaned against a tree trunk and wondered vaguely why she had to *try* to appear calm! They were just sitting—just resting.

"Look at that mountain."

She jumped at the sound of his voice.

He turned toward her, heedless of her unease as he went on, "With the sun reflecting off the glaciers, it's beautiful."

In a conscious effort to relax, she stretched her legs out before her and looked up at the glistening peak. "Uh huh." He was right. It was beautiful, but she just wasn't in the proper mood for appreciating nature's wonders just now. Wade's presence beside her was making her terribly uneasy. She cast a surreptitious glance toward him through lowered lashes.

His mouth was slanted in a crooked smile as he questioned, "Uh huh? Is that all you can say?" As he talked, he pulled his knee up, draping an arm around it. In an odd fascination, she watched his muscular calf flex with the movement. She liked the yellow gold shorts and shirt he was wearing. Their bright color contrasted nicely with his deep tan. Without much thought about their fledgling conversation, her mind more on the man than on her words, she asked, "What did you expect me to say?"

He moved his shoulders. "I don't know." Lifting those dark, beautifully fringed eyes back up toward the Denali peak, glistening in the late-morning sun, he improvised. "Something like, 'Its quiet wonder empties me of everyday cares.'" He swept an arm in a broad arc toward the mountain. "Or maybe, 'The sight of it leaves the mind receptive to the miracle of its timeless world.'" He sat back, shifting his body slightly so that he could better look down at her. Smiling ruefully, he challenged softly, "There. Now, don't you think that would have been better than 'uh huh'?"

Surprised by his unexpected eloquence, she forgot her earlier nervousness and shook her head, laughing. "That's awfully poetic talk for a *cop,* Wade." She lifted a skeptical chin. "Where did you read it—*National Geographic* magazine?"

For a split second, he looked like someone had thrown ice water in his face—or did he? The impression of hurt passed so quickly that she couldn't be positive she'd seen it at all.

He watched her quietly for a moment through slightly narrowed eyes. Then, exhaling wearily, almost regretfully, he rubbed a fist across his chin. In the quiet gap between gusts of wind, she could hear the sound of his knuckles grazing the beginnings of a new day's growth of beard. As she watched, he lifted a dark brow at her. "Did I promise to be on my best behavior if you promised to rest five minutes?"

She was taken somewhat off-guard by the question. "Uh—" Lifting a shoulder, she gave an unsure answering smile. "Yes, I guess."

He nodded. Silky noticed that his jaw had

begun flexing in irritation. "Would you say it's been five minutes yet?"

"Well—" What did he want her to say? "Not quite."

He shifted his eyes away and stood up, brushing grass from his shorts. The abruptness of his movement startled her. "Mind if we call it five?" he began crisply. "Maybe we'd better get going before I say something I regret." Reaching down, he took her arm and pulled her to her feet.

As soon as she was standing, he let her go, and Silky had the feeling that even that short contact had been too long to suit him. Without further comment, Wade walked briskly to his bike. Hurriedly, she moved up beside him, flicking her kickstand away from the ground. Lashes lowered, examining her white tennis shoes, she mumbled something that she hoped sounded like a positive response. She couldn't imagine what she had done to make him treat her so—so *coldly* all of a sudden. Any minute now she expected him to turn around and ask to see her driver's license!

"I'll lead. Try to stay in my wind shadow."

She blinked misty green eyes at him. "Your what?" It came out a little brokenly.

He glanced down at her, something vaguely akin to disappointment in his dark eyes. "Wind shadow. It means the same thing as drafting." One corner of his mouth lifted in a melancholy smile. "And—no. I didn't read that in the *National Geographic*."

Breaking their thoroughly disturbing eye contact, Wade swung his leg over the bike. Settling on the saddle, he pushed harder than necessary on his high pedal, propelling himself forward with a vengeance. Either he assumed Silky would follow, or he didn't care if she did, because he didn't look back.

Chapter Four

$\mathscr{B}$ack so soon?" Annie asked over her shoulder, then continued without waiting for an answer, "You'll notice that after all Rex's yammering about going too slow, we're not exactly whizzing along at the speed of sound." She let out a disdainful laugh. "But the *good* news is, after facing that head wind for a few hours, Rexie-boy'll be too tired to be his obnoxious self tonight!"

Silky, still trailing, grimaced at Annie's sarcasm as Wade interjected, "I saw our trucker friend parked at a truck stop about two miles back."

"You mean the guy with the fist?" Annie nodded, her red plastic helmet flashing reflected sunlight with the movement. "Yeah. Passing

71

that place was the *only* time Rex got up a really good head of steam!"

Silky thought she could hear a low chuckle as Wade pulled farther onto the shoulder, out of the line of bikers. Motioning her forward, he slowed until they were riding abreast, looking over at her for the first time since they had left the field some twenty minutes ago. His strong-boned face was bland, his dark eyes strangely seductive. They were devoid of anger—or, she was unaccountably distressed to note, any particular interest. "Move on up. I'll take the tail position," he directed quietly before slowing further and pulling in behind her.

She didn't have time to open her mouth until he was at her back, so she just kept it closed. A tremor of apprehension slid up her spine at having him back there. She wasn't sure why. Maybe she just didn't want to do anything foolish in front of him—literally. He was already irritated with her, and was probably just waiting for her to do something wrong so that he could act superior!

Of course, she'd done fine so far, managing to stay in the tight pack without doing anything to hurt herself or anyone else. There was no reason to believe she couldn't continue to do as well. Besides, she vowed as her hands tightened around her taped handlegrips, if a thirteen-year-old child could keep up, so could she!

Moments passed. Uncomfortable moments. *How irritating*, Silky thought. She was positive she could feel Wade staring at her. Swallowing hard, she shifted in her saddle, trying to get more comfortable. Highly distressed by her over-active imagination, she berated herself. *You can't feel a look, dummy!* It was a ridiculous idea, one unworthy of her. But worthy or no, she did feel his stare. It burned through the wispy pink nylon, at first just below her shoulder-blades. Then it moved down, warming her hips with the heat of a flamethrower through a spi-derweb. She tried to think of other things: of the fragrant crimson blur of wild cranberries that blanketed a cool tundra valley they were pass-ing; of the majesty of Denali, receding into the distance. But no matter how she tried to turn her thoughts away, she couldn't shake the eerie feeling of being so closely watched that it was having a peculiar warming effect on her skin—a tingling warmth that had nothing to do with the radiant heat of the sun beating down overhead.

Lunch was a brief scurry of buying at a tiny mom-and-pop grocery where canned fruit juice, packaged nuts and fresh fruits were grabbed up with the gusto of children given free rein in a candy store.

"Hey, Sil!" Rex called from the front door, propped open to catch the breeze. "Leonard is going to take our picture."

Picking up her change and slipping it into the tiny nylon pocket inside her waistband, Silky grabbed her apple juice, banana and bag of dried fruit and nut trail mix. "Okay," she agreed, "but first let's find a shady spot to put the food." Breezing out into the bright sunshine, she squinted as she looked around. "And I'd like to get this helmet off for at least *one* picture." Motioning with an elbow, she indicated a lone spruce that didn't have a milling group of hungry bikers clustered beneath it. "What about that one?"

"Good." Rex turned to where Leonard was uncasing his camera. "Len, the blue spruce by the corner."

Silky had just put down her lunch and slid her helmet strap over her handlebars when Leonard and Annie strolled up. Annie was munching from a can of macadamia nuts. She'd taken off her helmet, too, as had most everyone. "Okay," she announced, "camera crew's here. Where do we set up?"

Ignoring her joking question, Rex raised a mocking brow, intoning loftily, "Macadamia nuts? Well, aren't we the gourmet." There was just a touch of superior smirk quivering about his lips.

Annie's hazel eyes narrowed slightly, but she retained a pleasant enough expression. Nevertheless, Silky sucked in an uneasy breath. You could never predict what might happen when these two got within strangling distance of each other.

Nonchalantly, Annie popped several nuts into her mouth. "I'm proud of you, Rex," she mumbled. "I didn't know you could read words with nine letters."

Rex smiled coldly. "You know, Annie dear,

since you are what you eat, besides *nuts*, you must have a fondness for frogs' legs."

Annie made a mockery of what a smile was supposed to be. "Rex, darling? Did you know that, raised up on your hind legs like that, you look *almost* human?"

Silky, tensed for disaster, caught Rex's hand in both of hers, feeling it turn into a fist within her fingers. At the same instant, Silky heard Leonard ask rather anxiously, "Say, Ann! Uh—I just remembered, I forgot to load my camera. The film's in my handlebar bag. Could you get me a roll?" With his last words, he took her by her stiffened shoulders and gently propelled her away.

Turning toward Rex, Silky's mind fumbled wildly for a safe topic. Film? Pictures? "Rex?" She gingerly patted his fist before sliding her hand up to take his wrist. "Let's decide where to stand for the shot."

He turned slowly, mechanically, but when his eyes settled on her face, his expression lost its stoniness. "What is it, Sil?"

She smiled, relieved that, once again, the "Annie-Rex" megaton bomb had been successfully defused. "Do you want the picture in front of the grocery store? I mean how often does a person get to shop in 'Grizzly Joe's Quick Go'?" She pointed toward the dusty storefront window. "And those old metal signs for products of the twenties. They're wonderful."

Leonard interrupted in a voice that was louder

than necessary. "Well! For goodness sake, I *do* have film in this thing after all." Turning and waving an arm toward Annie, he shouted, "Say, Toone, I've got film here. Just sit down and have some of my herb tea." Brushing a hand through his oversized moustache, he added with forced casualness, "I'll be right there."

Annie glowered back at them, but to her credit, she didn't advance for another attack.

"Oh? A picture. Good idea, Huff." It was Wade's unmistakable baritone. "Everybody! Leonard's going to get a shot of us in front of the store."

Amid laughter and jovial shoving for position, Rex was pushed away from Silky. Annie, seemingly recovered from her pique, hurried over to act as stage director. "Okay Randy, kneel by your daddy there in front. Now you two smile! Well, that's fair. No, Beth. You and Dan quit kissing." She rolled her eyes for an instant before going on, "Wade, you're okay there behind Silky." Her take-charge smile vanished, and she gestured broadly. "Rex, why don't you move waaaayyy over to the left there and squat down behind Mr. Grizzly."

Everybody laughed but Rex and Silky—and perhaps one other person. Wade was standing directly behind Silky and, though she could feel his breath against her hair, she could swear that she didn't hear him laugh.

Finally, when everyone was posed between Mr. and Mrs. "Grizzly Quick Go," both chubby, and both in overalls, Leonard snapped the photo.

A second picture was taken when a rattletrap pickup pulled in and its long-haired youthful driver, an Alaskan Aleut teenager, was convinced—for the price of a cold drink—to snap a frame with Annie squeezed unsmiling between Rex and Leonard in the middle of an otherwise happy-looking group.

Hours and hours, miles and miles later, with Wade leading, they wheeled into a wooded clearing where camp was quickly set up, jobs divided, and a bathing schedule devised. Tonight was special for Fairbanks, for it was the day that they celebrated the year's longest day by hosting a Midnight Sun baseball game with the local Gold Panners. They were one of the top nonprofessional teams in the country, and would play at midnight at the Growden Memorial Stadium without artificial light. Sag Pack planned to attend in force.

"If you think you're going to that baseball game, jive turkey, you'd better take a deep peek at that creek."

Silky had unrolled her bedroll and was zipping up her tent when she heard the unmistakable "disk-jockeyese" of Mr. Douglas, Randy's father.

"Awe, Ice Man, I ain't dirty."

"Oh yeah? Well, if you're not, you're doing a pretty good imitation of it." Silky stole a look through her lashes as the elder Douglas lifted his mirrored sunglasses to squint at the boy. He exhaled rather tiredly. "Look, kid. I gotta sit next to you, so give me a break, and scrub." He pushed his glasses back into place on his slightly bent nose and gave Randy a swift swat on his cutoffs-clad backside, raising a puff of dust.

Randy screwed up a freckled scowl, baring oversized front teeth. "I'll get you for this, man."

"Yeah? Something else you learned from your mom?"

Silky's eyes widened, surprised by the definite edge that had come into Mr. Douglas's voice.

He tossed his plastic soap container after Randy. "Go scrub! I'll be there in a sec." Running his fingers through his shaggy mane of sandy hair, he paused by Silky, who had now stood up and was brushing grass from her knees, trying not to appear as though she'd been eavesdropping. Tossing his towel across his shoulder, he extended a hand. "Hey."

Dusting off her hands, she took his. "Hello, Mr. Douglas."

"Call me Ice. Everybody who's anybody does." He squeezed her hand and let it go. "You ever catch my show? 'Ice Man Morning Drive' on WROK in Anchorage?"

She smiled apologetically, shaking her head. "I'm afraid not. My musical preference falls somewhere between Johnny Mathis and Johnny Cash."

He made a classic sour-lemon face and clutched at his heart. "*Mathis! Cash!* Hell, lady, that's the dreaded adult-music chasm! You fall into that and the next thing you know, you're wearing socks and buying station wagons!"

She laughed at his melodramatic exaggeration, countering, "But you're the one who's a dad."

He sobered at the mention of fatherhood, his features closing in a scowl. "Hey—no way. Not *this* lad. Not for long, anyway."

Silky frowned, confused. "What do you mean?"

He looked at her thoughtfully as he lifted his reflective glasses again. This time she could see his eyes plainly. Light-lashed and the gray color of roadside snow, they seemed too sad for his twenty-some-odd years. She doubted that he was any older than she, but, still, there were definite wrinkles etched into the corners of his eyes, deep creases that had not been carved by laughter.

"Say," he asked quietly, apparently having made a decision. "Do you mind if I unload something on you?"

Silky was surprised and a little unnerved by his inquiry. Sweeping her gaze away from his doleful eyes, she offered tentatively, "I—I don't mind, I guess."

"I wouldn't bother you with this, but the kid—Randy—well, he's bad-mouthed about everybody on this trip except you, so I thought he might listen to you."

"Listen? To me?" Silky shifted uncertainly. "What is it that you want him to hear from me?"

Dropping his glasses back into place he looked around. Silky looked around, too. People were busy with the fire detail, dinner detail and general cleaning up. They were all too preoccupied with other things to eavesdrop. He motioned toward a spot under some pines where the bikes were parked. "What say we sit down?"

She nodded silently.

With long, disjointed strides, he beat her to the shaded area and spread his towel for them both. He rubbed his crooked nose then started, "Well, this is the deal. A little over a year and a half ago, I met Belle. She was this beautiful, young-looking lady of thirty-three. You know, the older-wiser type." He was speaking slowly now, and Silky had the feeling that he was no longer looking at her, but backward into his past, at the face of another woman. But not one he loved, not anymore anyway.

His features were cast in a harsh mask, his low recital no less sharp-edged as he explained, "She jerks my heart around and I marry her." Lifting his hands in a gesture of helplessness, he exhaled heavily. "Next minute, I'm daddy to this big-eyed twelve-year-old kid." He stopped, and Silky watched as his pent-up anger throbbed visibly in his temples.

Dropping his head, he began to toy with a sprig of grass as he took up the thread of his story. "Then, Belle wants us to be a *proper* family, you know—same last names and all? So I go the whole route and adopt the little anchor." With a sharp yank that made Silky jump, he uprooted a blade of grass. Raising his face back to hers, he snarled under his breath. "The ink wasn't dry on those damn adoption papers before Belle runs out on us! And *me*? I'm left with the kid." He lifted a hand to his hair and jerked his fingers through it. Silky noticed that his hand was trembling badly. "*Dammit!* I'm not *old* enough to have a thirteen-year-old kid! I was only fifteen when he was born!" Ice's voice broke in anguish as he poured out his painful, frightened admission.

"Your wife ran out on Randy!" Silky shook her head sadly. What was the matter with people these days—always running out on each other? Knowing that there was really little that she could do to console Ice, she patted his hand, offering hopefully, "Maybe she'll come back."

He snorted, his whispered answer rasping sharply against her face. "Yeah! No way. She's gone for good and I'm stuck with Randy. Why'd she pick me to dump the kid on? I'm too young to take on a half-grown boy!"

Silky clutched her hands together in her lap. "What are you going to do?"

"I'm taking him on this trip to—well—he likes riding his bike and camping, and I want to make the news as easy on him as I can. And the news is . . ." He cleared his throat with some difficulty. "I found out that Belle's got a second cousin living near Whitehorse. So, I figured I'd use this trip to sort of break it to the kid that I can't keep him, and then drop him off with her."

Silky heard a low, disbelieving sound and

realized with a start that it had come from deep in her own throat. She bit her lip as Ice hurried on.

"Even though Randy doesn't know this woman, he's not dumb. He'll see it's better this way."

Remembering those big sad eyes, Silky wondered how it must have hurt him, at his age, to have been tossed out like yesterday's garbage by his mother. Her question was low and unsteady. "You're leaving Randy with someone he doesn't even know? You're running out on him, too?"

Ice's face drained of color, his mouth hardening in a line of unshakable resolve. "It's all I can do; don't you see that? Besides, he'll be with blood kin."

She turned away, blinking out into the distance, trying not to think of Randy's unsmiling little face. A marsh hawk dipped into her line of vision and she followed its flight skyward. Though the bird soared with lofty, spirited freedom, its solitary celebration in the sky did nothing to lift Silky's forlorn spirit. She now understood what Ice wanted her to tell Randy. Shaking her head, she whispered, "You want *me* to tell Randy you're deserting him." It came out in a resigned sigh.

"Lord!" He groaned miserably. "Don't say it like that."

Silky spun to face him, her narrowed eyes sparking, critical. "I've never heard of anything so cowardly in my life! How could you ask this of me? The *least* you owe him is to tell him your-self!"

He laughed bitterly. "Yeah, sure. But, what you *should* do, and what you *can* do—it ain't always the same thing!" He lifted his glasses and rubbed roughly at his eyes, the act of a man trying not to cry. He croaked raggedly, "Look . . . lady. You can't call me anything I haven't already called myself." She watched his lips tremble as he stammered. "Ju—just be his friend, will you? Then, maybe—maybe later? It doesn't have to be this week, or even next week. Just tell him sometime before we get to White-horse."

Silky slumped back, closing her eyes. She felt wretched. The tree trunk was hard and unyield-ing, but no more so than she intended to be. "Now at least I know why he's been so unhappy. Poor kid . . . being abandoned by his mother." She felt a stab of dislike for this man, this quitter! It wasn't bad enough that he was a quitter, but he didn't even have the fortitude to *tell* Randy he was quitting. She gritted her teeth. A firm *no* was poised on her lips. When she lifted her eyes toward his again, Ice's glasses were back in place, hiding his desolate eyes. But to her extreme distress, she saw a lone tear trailing down his grimy cheek, leaving its damp track in the dust. The firm *no* wavered without sound on her parted lips. *The man was crying!* She had never been able to bear seeing a man weep. A feeling of defeat washed over her. With an unsteady tremor in her voice, she whispered, "I . . . I'll get to know Randy, Mr. Douglas. Besides," she added with a touch of rancor, "—maybe he would be better off with this second cousin, anyway."

For a long, oppressively quiet moment, he stared at her, unmoving. She stared back, but all she saw was her own reflection in his glasses. She saw in doubled miniature what he saw; a flushed face closed in a contemptuous frown. Her expression spoke very clearly of her disapproval.

With a moist hand, he gripped her shoulder, muttering self-consciously, "Thanks, Mrs. O. You're good people." Nodding to further affirm his statement, he seemed too affected for any more words. Abruptly, he stood.

Avoiding his gaze, Silky stood too. There was nothing at all that she could think of worth saying, so she remained silent. With a quick swoop, Ice pulled his towel up from the ground and, slapping it nervously against his leg, he ducked under a low branch and walked away toward the creek. As he left her, Silky noticed that he was standing a little taller, while she suddenly felt very bent. But the pain in her back could not totally be attributed to the added weight of responsibility he had dumped on her.

Putting her hand to her lower back, she kneaded the sore muscles. All the crouching against the wind today had left her cringing at the idea of getting on that bike again to go into Fairbanks for the Midnight Sun baseball game.

All she wanted right now was to rest—to *sleep!* But, even that possibility seemed remote after her haunting conversation with Ice. Thinking about Randy, she doubted that she would get any sleep, either! Mumbling to no one in particular, she observed dryly, "It's been a great day."

Silky had always heard that a dip in a cold creek was supposed to revive a body, not aid in killing it off. Though she'd managed to survive the frigid dip, the very thought of the impending trip into Fairbanks made her feel faint.

Shaking her head wearily, she fluffed her still-damp hair as she walked to Annie's tent. Bending, and grimacing at the way her back muscles protested yet another forced folding of her torso, she called softly, "Annie? You in there?"

"Yeah, kid. Just glossing the old lips."

Silky straightened. "Makeup? You?"

A curly red head popped out of the end of the tent as Annie grinned at her friend. "Don't panic, hon. It's just medicated gloss. I've got chapped lips." She crawled out and zipped up the opening. As she stood, she looked at Silky's attire for the first time. "Hey, you can't go to the game in your shorty robe. Better hurry and get dressed." She looked down at her wristwatch. "We're supposed to shove off in a minute."

Silky shrugged tiredly and sighed, rubbing a hand against the damp nape of her neck. "Annie, I couldn't get back on that bike today if you paid me. Honestly, I just can't understand why I'm having so much more trouble than anybody else on this trip—even Randy is doing better than I am." She shook her head and sighed disheartenedly at her admission of failure.

Annie lifted her brows sheepishly and shrugged. "Well, kid, to be honest, you shouldn't feel *that* distressed about it, really. Sag's not quite the group of beginners I told you it was."

Silky cocked a quizzical brow. "Not quite? How 'not quite,' Annie?"

The redhead made an uncomfortable grimace, avoiding Silky's narrowed eyes by scouting the higher branches of a pine tree. "Uh . . . well, pretty darned 'not quite.'"

When Annie's gaze fluttered down for an appraising look, Silky glared at her. "I hope you're not going to tell me anything I'll be forced to break your freckled neck for!"

Annie held up a halting hand, waving it in the negative. "Don't overexert yourself on my account. The ugly truth is that everybody in Sag— but you, that is—belongs to our bikers' club."

"I knew that."

"Yes—well, what you may not know is that we're all pretty salty bikers, if I do say so myself —even Randy. Or should I say *especially* Randy. Kids! They're all muscle. No fat. No sense. They never quit." She tried for lightness with a chuckle.

Jaws locked in irritation, Silky urged stonily, "Go on."

"Well—uh." Annie's smile waned and she

tugged at her ear as she went on, "Actually, Silk, this isn't really the sort of trip beginning bikers usually take. Even though I didn't know everyone in the group, I did know they're all seasoned bikers who decided to ride Sag to get a little more sightseeing in. Even so, our pace has been pretty darn brisk for most beginners."

Silky's stare was sharp and unswerving, like the steadily held blade of a knife. "Pretty *damn* brisk, you mean! Why didn't you tell me this before!"

Picking a piece of pine needle from Silky's robe, Annie ignored her friend's anger, answering in a motherly tone, "You know, kiddo, when you get tired, you get a little cranky. I've been meaning to talk to you about that." She patted Silky's shoulder in an impudent attempt at camaraderie. "Just look at it this way. You ought to feel pretty good about keeping up as well as you have. You're a real trooper!"

"Well, if I'm a trooper, then you'll have to admit that Rex is absolutely fantastic. He's keeping up, and he just joined the club for this trip."

Annie let out a cracking laugh. "Oh, he's fantastic all right, if *he's* any judge. Besides, I hear skirt chasers have to keep in pretty good shape."

Silky groaned, throwing up her hands in total frustration. "Annie, you know I love you like a sister, but sometimes you can be a royal pain in the neck!"

"You have a much higher opinion of her than I do, Sil," Rex broke in, a definite sarcastic edge to his voice.

Both women turned to see him walking toward them. When he got near enough, he reached out and lightly traced Silky's nose with a finger. "Trouble in paradise?"

Annie purred near his right elbow, "Well now, if that wasn't straight from the horse's mouth." The corners of her lips lifted maliciously. "For once, Rex, you're the *front* end!"

Hastily, Silky moved between them, taking each by an arm. "Look you two, do you mind if we call this one a draw? I'm awfully tired."

Annie took pity. "You let go so that I can get the circulation back in the old fingers, and it's a deal."

Silky dropped her hands as Annie continued, "Now, back to your dragging little tail. If you're too pooped to go, then don't. No problem."

"What's this?" Rex asked. "You're not feeling well?" He held her shoulders, his eyes narrowing with concern. She smiled at his interest, noticing how attractive he looked in his emerald green biking shirt and shorts. The words *Alaskan Sport* were spelled out in navy between two diagonal silver stripes across his chest. His shoes, too, were emerald with silver accent stripes. The only part of his wardrobe that remained the same from day to day was his tan safety helmet.

He was so tall, so athletically slender, and his cleanshaven face was so dashingly angular, that the sight of him standing there nearly took her breath away. "Oh, I'm okay, Rex, just beat."

Cocking his blond head in that jaunty way he had, he squeezed her shoulders reassuringly. "Well, don't worry. I'll stay here with you. I certainly couldn't enjoy the game, thinking about you being out here all alone."

"She won't be, Rex. But, thanks anyway."

Both Silky and Rex raised their heads simultaneously at the sound of Wade's baritone. Annie turned too, speaking first. "Hi, Wade. How's the leg?"

"Mediocre, thanks." He walked forward the few remaining feet to join them and Silky noticed that his limp was much more pronounced than it had been that morning. It looked as though his day of leading the tight pack in the high winds had done his leg some real harm. "Wade," she said, "you need to get some heat on that."

His smile was easy. "I plan to. So, you see, Rex"—he shifted his eyes almost reluctantly away from Silky. "You don't need to stay. You go on and have a good time."

"Now just slow down a minute."

Annie waved, interrupting. "Wade, let me take it," she offered pleasantly, almost too pleasantly. "Okay, Rex, read my lips. Wade said, 'Go . . . on . . . and . . .'"

"That's not what I meant and you know it!" Rex shot at her before turning to Wade. "I'm staying! End of discussion!"

Annie shook her curly head. "Look, Rex.

There's nothing I'd like better than to have you here at camp and out of my hair. But, somebody needs to remind you about just why you're on this little jaunt—publicity for the store, remember? Bread'n'butter time? Well, this game is going to have all kinds of press, both for the game and for the Biked-Alaska-thoners."

As Silky watched, Rex's scowl softened at Annie's words. "Besides, they've got special bleachers set up for us, probably even be some interviews." She paused. Rex's face was now clearly registering the business implications of making an appearance at the game. Annie added with a trace of forced enthusiasm, "That outfit of yours would sure show up well on color TV, don't you think?"

Standing stiff and tense, Silky was feeling worse for some odd reason. Her back throbbed. Part of her added distress, she was sure, was the discovery that Wade would be there in camp, *alone,* with her for most of the night. Tension raised her voice an octave as she asked, "Who's going to lead if Wade doesn't go?" Knowing how his leg must be hurting him, Silky didn't begrudge him his right to stay in camp and nurse those overworked muscles; but still there was a tiny hope—way down in her toes—that somebody would suggest that since the leader couldn't go, maybe it would be better if nobody went.

"I'd asked Annie to think about leading for me." Wade patted the redhead's shoulder. "Besides, somebody needs to stay here to watch the camp. Since I can't ride, it might as well be me."

"I can stay and watch it," Silky offered a little too enthusiastically.

Annie dusted her hands together, a look of satisfaction on her expressive face. "Good, you'll both stay. Maybe between the two of you we can come up with one healthy person. "C'mon Rex. Let's round up the stragglers. We've got a ball game to bilk for all the hype it's worth."

Giving a resigned shrug, Rex turned to follow Annie with a final helpless glance at Silky. He was going.

Crossing her arms beneath her breasts, Silky exhaled heavily and ventured, "Well, what do I do? Patrol the perimeter?"

"You could." There was a brief moment when he just stood there smiling down at her. "Is that what you want to do?"

She dropped her eyes to her slippered feet. "Actually, I really just want to go to bed." Her long lashes fluttered back up to meet his gaze straight on. "But if I'm needed to do something, I'll do it. I feel badly enough about not having the wherewithal to make the game."

Smiling, he shook his head. Somehow, it seemed like a reassuring gesture. "You're doing great, Silky. By next week, you'll be keeping up just fine." Reaching out, he touched her jaw with a finger, sliding it down to her chin. "If you want to go to bed, go on. The camp will be fine."

She moved slightly, lifting her chin from his

soft touch. Her eyes slid away from his face, and the unbidden thought that he was strikingly handsome in blue skitted through her consciousness as she realized he was wearing the same light blue shirt and hip-caressing navy pants he had worn the first day of the trip—the day he had kissed her. She felt her cheeks go fiery hot with the memory.

Pulling a hand through her hair, she murmured, "I—I think I'll just turn in. Good night, Wade." Without waiting for a reply, she picked her way through the maze of colorful tents back to hers, and ducked inside.

Lying on her back, she listened to the bustle of departing bikers. Nearly a quarter of an hour later, she was still lying there, wide awake, hearing nothing but the occasional ghostly, nocturnal question of a short-eared owl as he called out in the dusky wilderness night, "Whoooo? Whoooo?"

Who? No. That wasn't the right question. The question, at least as far as Silky was concerned, was *what*? What was making her feel so guilty? It wasn't the fact that she was a bike-a-thon failure. Both Annie and Wade had put her at ease there. Neither was it that she had gone to bed and left Wade alone to watch the camp. He'd said it was okay. Well . . . maybe she did feel a little guilty about that. After all, Wade was hurting too.

She sat bolt upright. That was it! She could have helped him with his leg, and she hadn't offered to do a single thing! Filled with resolve, she reached for her bag of toilet articles, grabbing a bottle of aspirin and a squeeze tube of lotion.

Seconds later, she'd scrambled out of her tent. Wincing at the pain involved in straightening up, she looked around. Wade was sitting on his bedroll beside the flickering fire, a pan of steaming water on the ground beside him. With a slight intake of breath, she noticed that he had removed his shirt in the fire's radiant heat. Wavering firelight reached out and caught in its bright aura the red gold highlights of the curling hair that lay close and protective over the corded muscles of his chest.

Her eyes moved slowly up to note that even his black hair glowed an intriguing, unexplainable golden red where the firelight touched it in the dancing reflection of the low flames. It surprised her to see that a man so dark by day could yield such an enticing variance of color in the deceptive shimmer of a fire.

As she watched his profile, he began to knead his scarred calf. He'd certainly had a rough day making it easier for everyone else in the pack, and he was paying for it now. A pang of sympathy pricked her as she watched him.

She'd thought her approach had been practically soundless, but when she reached him, he glanced over his shoulder, raising sparkling black eyes to hers. "Hi. I thought you'd gone to bed."

"I did." Holding out the bottle of aspirin, she began, "But it occurred to me you might need

this." Her brief explanation came out a bit briskly, and she felt strangely timid all of a sudden.
She forced a small smile, reminding herself that
she was doing the right thing—finally.

"Thanks." He flashed her a lopsided grin and
patted the bedroll. "Join me? A fire's nicer with
company."

Chapter Five

Well . . ." She hesitated as she watched him work at easing his damaged leg. But it was only a few seconds before she made her decision. "I will, if you let me massage your gastrocnemius." Making a circling motion with her hand, she directed, "Turn over and I'll work the stiffness out."

His smile turned to a devilish grin. "If the gastrocnemius is what I hope it is, I won't have to turn over for you to work the stiffness out."

Unable to keep from grinning at his bald-faced innuendo, she shook her head as though he were a hopeless case. "Settle down, big boy. I was talking about your calf muscles. Then I'll wrap your *leg* in a hot towel. With the aspirin, you should be much better by morning."

He stopped what he was doing and looked up

at her, his expression questioning. "You're serious, aren't you?"

"I wouldn't have offered if I weren't."

Dark eyes lingered curiously on her face for a moment before his features relaxed in an easy smile. Without further need for coaxing, he turned to lie prone, resting his chin on his hands. He looked back over his shoulder toward her, his grin lopsided and openly suggestive. "I'm all yours, but I'm at a slight disadvantage on my stomach."

His highly communicable charm gave her no choice but to laugh. "That's reassuring." She knelt down beside him and pushed a wispy strand of hair behind her ear. To get better situated, she straddled his leg with her knees and picked up the tube of lotion.

"What's reassuring, the fact that I'm all yours?" he probed, humor glistening in his eyes.

"No." She rubbed lotion on her hands.

Undaunted, he went on conversationally, "You know what it means when a woman straddles a man's leg, don't you?"

She shot him a look through narrowed eyes. "It means she's got no place to sit."

"Nope. Means she's interested in him and she wants to be ravished. In Hawaii women tell a man the same thing with a flower behind one ear." He settled back down. With his cheek on his hands, he focused on the darkened distance. It looked as though he was really planning to have a good time with her about this whole situation.

Pretending total nonchalance, she leaned forward and placed her palms on either side of his granitelike calf. "And just *who* says that?"

"Let's put it this way. I've never heard the hypothesis questioned."

With the heels of her hands, she pressed upward, moving slowly along the back of his leg. "Well, consider it questioned."

He glanced back over his shoulder, eyes narrowed in exaggerated disbelief. "Do you mean to tell me that you're going to fly in the face of tradition?"

"And peck out its little eyes."

"Wild-eyed radical." He flashed her a highly amused smile before lying back down.

With a playful punch to the back of his leg, she admonished, "Oh, just hush and relax your leg muscles."

"The woman's a radical *and* a bully," he mumbled as though he were talking to himself.

Biting her lips between her teeth, she suppressed a giggle. "Sorry. Let me know if I get too rough for you."

"You'll know by the way I flip you to your back and have my way with you."

"Oh good. I don't mind corrective criticism as long as it's subtle." She was playing along now, remaining conversational as she halted the forward motion just below his knee. Repeating the procedure, she began to move slowly back down over the solid, scarred calf. The light furring tingled against the palms of her hands. His calf was like a rock. It was easy to see—or feel—that he'd worked very hard to bring his leg back to its fullest potential. But the damage to the tissue had been severe, and it was unlikely that his strength would ever be as it had once been, no matter how he tried.

While she continued to massage, her eyes slid to his naked back. He was lying quite still now. Tanned as he was, in the flutter of firelight, he looked like a bronze statue, some ancient Greek deity at rest after a wearing day of fighting with lance and shield. His back was lean and broad, and her eyes ran with fascination over the contours of muscles and sinew. Though the flesh looked like bronze in the capricious light, she knew it wouldn't feel cold. Certainly his leg, though hard as metal, was responsive, even yielding.

She wondered idly if his back, powerful-looking even in repose, would feel as supple, yet vital as she imagined it would. She was abruptly drawn out of her unconscious wanderings when she heard Wade clear his throat a bit more loudly than necessary. He shifted slightly before speaking her name in an oddly hoarse question. "Silky?"

She blinked back to reality and lifted her head to his profile. He had raised up on an elbow, and his face was serious as he began in a strained voice, "If the idea of massaging me is to help me forget the pain in my calf, it's working. If you've got something more than a massage in mind, just say so."

She frowned, confused not only by what he

was saying, but by the husky way he was saying it. Dropping her gaze to the place where her hands rested, she was shocked to see that she had unconsciously massaged her way up his leg until her fingers were barely beneath the edge of his shorts. Without realizing it, she'd come dangerously close to the tight, rounded rise of his buttocks.

"Oh!" She jerked her hands from beneath his biking shorts. "Oh, my goodness, Wade. I'm sorry. My mind must have been wandering."

His lips parted in a grin ripe with charming menace. "Mine definitely was. Do you want to know where?"

She could tell that he was only half-teasing now. At least she hoped that it was closer to half than to zero. This wasn't a good place to be alone with a big, strong, amorous bear of a man when he got *that* look in his eyes—no matter how attractive the eyes. Fortunately, she was a big girl. She knew that men were not hard to handle if you refused to take them seriously. "I think I'll wait for the movie, thanks," she said, smiling.

"Chicken." His lips twitched with humor as he turned away and lowered himself back to the bedroll. "Actually, I think you already know. You're just avoiding the subject."

She sniffed derisively. "Do *you* know that ever since I met you, you've made comments like that. Just what makes you think you know so much about everything?"

He chuckled, and even in her aggravated state, she found the masculine sound of his

laughter unexpectedly pleasant. As she
watched, he flexed his back muscles with an
easy shrug. "It's really nothing. I've got this
psychic thing."

"Well, don't show it to me."

"Not even in the movie?" he interjected with
mock concern.

Keeping her lips firm, she vowed to herself
that he was absolutely not going to make her
laugh. With less-than-gentle pressure, she
pressed her thumbs into his calf and moved
them in a revolving motion. Through clenched
teeth she gritted, "Is this better?"

"Yes"—a deep, vaguely regretful chuckle em-
phasized the pause—"and no. But, you might do
well to remember what I said I'd do with you if
you got too rough."

She squeezed, kneading the leg. Even though
she was fairly certain he was kidding, she eased
up a bit. Feeling silly, she countered flippantly,
"Oh, Wade, I couldn't hurt you if I tried."

Lifting his chin a fraction, he watched her
silently for a moment out of the corner of his eye.
"Don't bet on it, lady." The amused sparkle that
had seemed so at home there was gone now, but
before she could worry over his odd remark, he
lowered his head to the bedroll and remarked
casually, "You're good with your hands. Do you
do this sort of thing as part of your job?"

"No. My dad was a farmer in Kansas. A tractor
accident nearly crippled him when he was a boy.
He got the use of his legs back, but sometimes,

after he got older, they pained him. After Mother died, I used to do this for him when he felt really bad."

"I see." He turned again, laying his cheek on a fist. Where's your dad, now?"

She paused, looking up at nothing in particular. "He died a few months after I married Rex."

"I'm sorry." He sounded as though he really was.

She shrugged her shoulders. "Thanks, but it was a long time ago. I have my memories." They were quiet for a moment as she stroked his calf, pressing firmly into the scarred flesh. "Wade, how did you hurt your leg?" She hardly realized she had asked the question before she heard herself speak it.

"It's not a great story."

She smiled apologetically and began her forward kneading motion again. "That's okay. If you'd rather not talk about it, just say so. But, it's really not just idle curiosity. Working in Emergency has cured me of that."

"I can imagine." Looking into the darkness beyond the fire, he began, "It was in Detroit; my last undercover job." He flicked a quick look back. "Remember in the hospital, when you believed I was the bad guy?"

She nodded, not particularly pleased at the reminder.

"Well," he explained quietly, "some of the less subtly oriented Motor City underworld *didn't* believe that Joe, my partner, and I were—bad guys, that is. So they decided to make a serious point with the Detroit Police Department by ramming our car with a stolen garbage truck."

Silky came to a dead halt as he continued, "They hit us broadside. Joe's side. I was lucky. I spent six months in the hospital."

"And Joe?" she asked, barely breathing.

"Never even made it to the hospital." He stopped talking, and she could see an angry pumping of muscle in his jaw. "That—among other things—helped me decide to come here. Lost my taste for undercover work."

Totally forgetting her job as a masseuse, Silky slid off of him and came down on her stomach beside him. "Wade, you were working undercover when I met you."

He grinned as she joined him on the blanket. "Hi, there. What do I owe you?"

When she realized where she was, she laughed aloud. "Oops. I'm not finished, I just—" She started to get back up, but he restrained her with a gentle hand on her wrist.

"The leg is perfect, Silky." He moved to sit up. "And to answer your question, yes. I was working undercover that night." He released her wrist as she sat up to face him. "It just happened that the detective I had working on the case called in sick with the mumps—caught them from his four-year-old. I'd just gotten back from a weekend of biking and was still pretty scruffy. Remember?"

She rolled her eyes. "Vaguely."

"I thought you might." His glance was mild

and friendly as he drew a knee to his chest and curled an elbow around it. "Since I knew the details of the job, I just took it myself." Shrugging, he added, "Wasn't supposed to be much to it."

Silky pursed her lips, nodding. "Yes. Poor Officer Taylor." She found herself wishing the detective with the mumps had been more resistant to the disease. At least, if she'd made a fool of herself in front of him, she wouldn't be spending a month in the woods with him now being reminded of it day after day! "And, I suppose you've sworn off undercover work again."

"Lieutenants rarely do undercover work. But, to be honest, I found that particular case quite rewarding." He picked up the tube of lotion. "Enough about business. Let me pay you back in kind for your massage; your back for my leg."

Her head shot up in surprise at his unexpected suggestion. "Oh"—she cleared her throat, which had gone prickly dry—"uh, no—I don't—that won't be necessary."

He interrupted. "Take off the robe, first, though." He was squeezing lotion into his palms, acting as though she had been thrilled with the idea rather than stuttering out weak, negative responses, as she was.

"But, Wade, I'm just wearing a T-shirt and—uh—"

He looked up as he capped the tube. "Panties?"

She nearly died of embarrassment, or she would have if her body had had any consideration of her feelings at all. It wasn't so much because he'd said the word *panties,* or even because she couldn't say it. It was because he'd said it so matter-of-factly, as if he'd said "roller-skates."

He was suggesting, casually, "I've seen you that way before, if you'll recall. But, if you'd feel better about it, just pull out of your sleeves and leave the robe tied at the waist. That way I can get to your back and you can still preserve your modesty."

He was talking as though the idea made perfect sense. So what if he had kissed her that first night? He'd been nothing short of a gentleman since. And, it was certainly true that her back would feel so much better with a little tender loving care—not much, mind you, but maybe just a little. After all, as he'd said, it would be payment in kind.

"Well . . ." she finally acquiesced, pulling her arms out of her sleeves. Her brows came together in a frown of consternation when she noticed how her breasts swayed liquidly with her movements, their tips pressing defiantly against the pink cotton of her shirt. Casting Wade a furtive glance, she couldn't tell if he'd been aware of her bouncing sway, or if he was as completely absorbed in rubbing the lotion into his hands as he appeared to be.

"Lie down on your stomach," he murmured quietly.

She did as she was told, feeling a little self-conscious and tense. As she cupped her chin in her hands, the thought crossed her mind to say, "I'm all yours," as he'd done earlier, but it would have been a joke with definite sexual overtones and Wade seemed inclined to take things so literally! Instead, she just said, "Okay, what now?"

"Now *you* relax," he answered as he moved to straddle her hips with his thighs. She could feel his solid warmth even through the terry of her robe as his knees pressed against the fleshy part of her hips. *And he expected her to relax?* Surely he could move his legs away from her just enough to put some space between them. She decided to suggest the possibility nicely, but directly. "Wade, I think—" She had just begun when his warm, lotion-covered hands slid under her T-shirt, stealing away her words in a surprised intake of breath.

"What do you think?" he asked as his long, powerful fingers spread, curling around her waist and kneading the tensed, aching muscles gently. Without giving her a chance to answer, he spoke again, "You're not relaxing, Silky. Think about something pleasant."

Pleasant! What could be more pleasant than the soothing massage from those able hands? But "pleasant" and "relaxing" were two different things in this case. "I'll try."

His thumbs were slowly circling either side of her spine, and she found herself unconsciously circling her lips with her tongue, matching his deliberate movements. Closing her eyes and moving her hands from her chin, she turned her face to her side. Laying her cheek on the cool blanket, she let out a sigh of contentment as the fatigue and stiffness drained away. After a minute—or possibly ten minutes, her fogged mind couldn't be sure—she heard Wade whisper her name, almost as though he were afraid of waking her. "Silky?"

She blinked heavy lids, but didn't quite get her eyes opened. "Hmmmmm?"

"Didn't Rex ever massage your back?" As he spoke, he slid his hands, palms spread, toward her shoulders. It felt so good that she breathed an audible sigh. What had he asked? Her eyes fluttered sleepily as she queried with a throaty, "Hummm?"

"Nothing." His fingers were kneading, pressing with firm but gentle authority. As his hands moved apart, his fingers, still working their warm miracles over her, dipped down her sides, lightly grazing the swell of her breasts. There, they lingered, tracing lightly along her sweetly feminine contours. His hands stilled, and as they did, she thought she heard him breathe her name. Or was it a velvety soft curse? Before she had time to consider which it had been she was brought fully awake when he jerked his hands away from her back, pulling the T-shirt down smartly over her tingling skin. She lost the warmth of his thighs against her hips as he rolled off of her and sat up, wrapping his arms stiffly about his knees, which were drawn up almost protectively to his chest. "Okay, Silky," he croaked, "that's it for me. A man can only take so much."

She pulled up on one elbow, staring apprehensively over at him, hunched there as though he were ill. "What?" she asked, sitting beside him. They were both facing the fire now, and she could see that his face was set in a troubled frown. "Are you sick, Wade?"

He closed his eyes, his expression remaining pained as he exhaled a long breath. When he finally looked at her again, his lips twisted in a humorless grin. "I had an attack just then, but I'll survive. Give me a minute."

"Attack?" She pulled her legs up under her and sat back on her heels. "Your leg?"

He snorted, shifting his ebony eyes toward the fire, giving them the red glow of burning coal. "No," he muttered, "plain old, physically debilitating lust." Inclining his head, he looked down at her and watched the gradual blossom of shock that widened her eyes and parted her lips. His smirk was charmingly wry. "I knew you'd be pleased."

With a few seconds to take the edge off of her astonishment, she felt herself relax a little. Squinting dubiously, she diagnosed. "You've just been on the road too long."

His smile softened slightly. "The *road* has nothing to do with it."

Strangely, she felt no threat from his unabashed honesty. Her lips twitched impudently, as she challenged, "So, an attack of lust does *that* to you?" She indicated his almost fetal position with an airy wave of her hand. "I have to tell you, Lieutenant, it's not a pretty sight."

"I'm sure. But it was either this, or storm your flimsy little terrycloth walls."

Undaunted, she shook her head, plunging on. "Cops don't storm women's walls against their will. They help women."

A heartbeat passed before he chuckled with soft irony. "Maybe—but, *I* damn well know I almost helped you out of your clothes." Leveling his dark eyes on her, he sobered as he reached out and took her wrist in the warm vice of his fingers. "You'd better hope you're right about cops." With his free hand on her shoulder, he pressed her down onto the bedroll.

Silky felt the quilt mold to her back, but she didn't struggle. "Wade?" she breathed. "What are you doing?"

Unsmiling, he shook his head. "I don't know," he murmured in a slightly unsteady voice that she hardly recognized to be his, and she couldn't help but believe him.

A surge of fear, mingled strongly with excitement, raced through her as she lay there staring up into the hypnotic darkness of his eyes. Somewhere in a small corner of her temporarily malfunctioning mind, a weak little voice railed on about curiosity and how it killed cats and foolish women. If he'd only said he was going to make love to her, she could have soundly rejected him. If he'd just admitted he was going to rape her, she could have fought with all of her strength. But he'd said he didn't know what he was going to do. And because he didn't know, it became imperative that she *did*. The heat she saw in his eyes didn't alarm her, though it probably should have. Yet she could have sworn that even in the smoky blackness, she could detect no violence. What then? Determination? Yes, but there was something else, something not quite readable. It had been there this morning when they had rested under the willows. She swallowed spasmodically. "Do—do you know yet?"

"No." He was leaning over her, one hand pinning her shoulder, the other holding her wrist to her side. Their eyes held, clung together, as the sensuous darkness of his gaze drew closer, becoming her total reality. In an almost soundless whisper, he teased her lips with his as he asked, "Did I thank you for the aspirin?" A gentle, brotherly kiss moistened the tip of her nose.

She lifted her chin slightly, her lips parting in an unconscious and very unsisterly invitation for him to place the same light gift lower. With a sigh that held her name, he accepted her tiny offering, molding his lips to hers. The kiss did not devour or consume, but merely taunted, so lightly that she lifted her face to meet his lips more firmly; to taste him to the fullest. Through languidly lowered lashes, she could see a pleasant upward turn at the corner of his lips. He moved his hand from her shoulder up to cradle the back of her head. Holding her securely, he laid final claim to her eagerly parted lips. It was an infinitesimal assertion of ownership, if one considered the vastness of the wilderness in which they lay. But the point was moot.

Silky's eyes were closed to the beauty of the endless wilds, her concentration centered only on the wild intimacy that he was unleashing within her body. She could not, would not, make herself aware of anything but the curious ease with which their lips fitted together. Odder still —because a kiss is a fluid, living thing—was the comfortable way they continued to come together. The joy of the contact did not lessen as the intimate ballet moved and changed, but increased and became even more pleasurable.

He nipped lightly at her upper lip, sending a renewed charge of feeling rushing through her, igniting a heated, liquid sensation in her stomach that spread like warm, sweet syrup through her body. Her lips fairly throbbed with it, and she parted them farther, inviting his exploration. Again he accepted, his tongue enticing, tempting, warming her more.

She felt the light tracing of his fingers as he slid his hand beneath her T-shirt, and caressed her rib cage below her breasts. He stroked as lightly with his fingertips as he did with his tongue, his thumb gently moving back and forth in the valley between her breasts. With each feathery caress of his fingers, she expected him to slip his hand up to capture her quivering fullness. But he did not. His fingertips grazed the barest rise of flesh so sensitive to a man's touch, tantalizing, promising, but he went no further. She thought she would go mad, wild with desire for him to hold her. The core of her being burned for the promises that he was so eloquently making to be kept.

Whimpering, she moved against him. It wasn't a planned thing. It was a necessary thing, a need that went beyond civilization— back, back to something very strong, very basic. "Wade . . ." She gasped as he lifted his scalding kiss from her lips. Taking his hand, she lifted it, and with trembling fingers, pressed it over her milky softness.

Silky felt a quick shiver wrack his body as he moaned, "My God, woman. Do you know what you're doing?"

"No." The word was a plaintive sigh as she rolled her head from side to side in a conscious effort to negate what her body was doing. Even so, she circled his back, sliding her hands up, then down, over the corded muscles that flexed beneath her urgent touch.

He stilled her head, kissing her jaw and tracing along the rapidly beating pulse in her throat with his tongue. She pulled him to her, and as he settled over her, she let out a short, sharp gasp to feel the full measure of his desire.

As he lifted his face to look into her eyes, he pulled her T-shirt up over her breasts, revealing them, at last, to his devouring gaze. "Silky, if

this is a dream, be kind and let me dream it."
His features lost their sharp edges. He was all
softness, all gentleness, and though he wasn't
smiling, and his shadowed face revealed a
vaguely haunted bleakness in the eyes, Silky
thought his face was the most beautiful sight
she could remember seeing. A smile parted her
lips and she lifted her hands to his thick, tousled
hair, lowering his marvelous, distracted face to
her waiting mounds of femininity, nipples
stretched taut in anticipation of his kisses.

He nuzzled her there and she loved the slight
roughness of his face. His tongue flicked at a
rosy nipple, inspiring a long, languid sigh of pure
ecstasy from her parted lips. At her response, he
put his arms about her, pulling her as close to
him as was humanly possible. "Let me love you,
Silky," he murmured, sliding one hand down to
cup her hip. Deft fingers curled under the sheer
fabric of her underpants to stroke the skin there.

Whispering against the delighted tip of her
breast, he said, "It's right. It has been since the
first night we met. You know it, don't you?" The
fingers that were hooked over the hip-hugging
band of her panties slowly began to move down
as he urged with a passion-thickened voice,
"Don't you, darling?"

She was weak with need for him. Feeling the
flimsy but very real barrier of lace being carefully disposed of, she tried to muster a vestige of
regret, but none would come. Her body needed
the things he was offering, and she was defense-

less against him. She hadn't, for one sane or insane instant, wanted to resist him. The tiny piece of lace that had been her clothes slipped easily over her knees and was gone. She didn't mourn its passing.

He took her hand and moved it to the fastening of his shorts. "When you're ready." He covered her hand reassuringly for a moment before moving to caress her thigh. Turning slightly, he placed his other arm firmly under her head, cradling her in the crook of his arm, holding her close. She kissed his chest and cuddled closer. Somehow she instinctively sensed what he would do now, and she moistened her lips in anticipation as his hand slid between her legs where he touched her ever so softly. She quivered and let her head fall back, closing her eyes to everything but the exquisite sensations he was eliciting with his gentle exploration. "You're a delight, Silky," he murmured into the shell of her ear. With a light kiss on her lobe, he touched her more intimately.

"Ohhh—oh Wade," she cried.

"Yes, love."

She moved against him, her desire so heightened that she could not stand being without him a moment longer. She became a part of the wild, untamed land in his arms, drawn unfathomably to the virile force that he was, a powerful wind that carried her where it willed. She tugged distractedly at his shorts, but he whispered, "Not yet, sweetheart." He hastened his movements, and she arched against him, whimpering her desire. "Wade—I want you so—so much."

"And I want you, beautiful Silky." He nipped at her ear. His breath tempted the sensitive skin, sending a sweet shock down her spine as expert hands sent surge after surge of white-hot sensations careening throughout her body. She felt as though he were tearing her apart, and it was a wonderful rending.

A breeze floated across them. Silky could feel its extreme coolness, and realized that she must be glistening with sweat as her body tensed, reaching desperately for the zenith of feeling that he was creating within her. Her breath was coming in short, panting cries, and she turned her face into Wade's chest, crying into the tangle of musky hair, "Wade—Wade!" With one final arch, her body quivered. The sigh that began deep in her throat was exhaled slowly with sweet ecstasy of feeling. Then, with a tingling warmth, the golden feeling began to drain away, leaving her sated and whole.

She let go of the bedroll she had been clutching and turned to Wade, kissing his chest and rubbing her face in the mat of softness. Another light kiss teased his nipple. With her fingers spread, she ran a hand through the vee of hair that ran up toward his chest. Feeling contented in his arms, she questioned, a little hoarsely, "Why?"

He shifted, and she fluttered a tentative, almost shy glance up at his face. He was smiling down at her. "Why what?" he coaxed, hugging her closer.

"You know why what. Why didn't you . . ." She stopped, unable to go on.

"I told you." His hands were caressing her back with silken strokes. "I wanted to make you happy."

She dropped her eyes as she toyed with the waistband of his shorts. Unable to stop herself, she mumbled, "Was it worth it?"

He chuckled, and she could feel the deep reverberation of his delight tickle her ear. "Of course. You make it sound like a sacrifice." He kissed her forehead and, as he turned her head up so that she could accept his next kiss on her lips, he whispered almost too softly for her to hear, "You're a beautiful woman." His hands, never still, were bringing freshly awakened nerve endings to life again as he took possession of her lips and did wonderful things to them.

Not recognizing the wanton woman who had taken over her body, Silky put her hands under the waistband of his shorts, and slowly began to pull them down. He lifted his hips to help, and she soon had him completely free of his clothes. Her eyes moved over the fully aroused length of him. In the waning glow of the fire he seemed more like a reclining heathen god, completely content with his dominion over this trackless wilderness. She pushed herself up to sit so that she could look down at him. As she lay both hands softly on his chest, her name floated up to her in a questioning whisper. She shook her head, quieting him. She closed her eyes. The memory of his puzzled expression lingered in her mind's eyes as she began to touch him. She had to know the feel of his flesh. Her hands slid down the hard, flat belly, and she heard him groan. He squeezed her shoulder for a moment before he let her go, allowing his hand to slide down her arm and drop to the bedroll.

Moving on in her quest, she took great care to explore every contour of his body. Even the furrowed scars on his calf sent a ripple of pleasure up her spine.

"Silky," he called, his voice husky with need. Opening her eyes, she looked down at him. His face was tense and, with his lashes lowered to watch her, she could see nothing of his dark eyes but an occasional liquid glisten. Lifting a hand toward her, he ordered softly, "Come here."

Willingly, she came into his arms. As he turned her onto her back, she opened herself to his passion with a relish that she would never have imagined. He had made her crave him. When they came together, he filled her beyond all her imaginings. The blossoming of primeval feelings in her core tore outward, thrilling her whole being, and she gasped. Opening her eyes wide, she looked up into his face. His eyes were closed, his features a mask of intense ardor. "Silky, Silky," he moaned as he began to move within her.

With every thrust he threw her into an unstable orbit somewhere beyond the heavens. He knew just how to touch a woman. His movements were deliberate, beginning very slowly and then building, until she was clinging to him and crying. She had never been this far before, in this rarefied atmosphere where there was little air, but an unimaginable amount of spectacular color and sensation. She let the last vestiges of control slide away, and she cried out into the vast night.

"O-O-Ohhh!" It was a half-sigh, half-moan as he drove himself faithfully home. Encircling her with his arms, he held her tightly, his body quaking with its own climax. She hugged his shuddering back and unaccountably began to sob into his shoulder, crying from the depths of her soul.

"Sweetheart?" he questioned, tasting the salty dampness on her face with gentling kisses. "Why tears?"

She squeezed her eyes shut and curled her legs possessively over his thighs, gasping. "I—I don't know. Just, hold me, please." Did she really not know, or did she just not want to know?

He brushed a damp strand of hair away from her cheek and nuzzled the place it had been, whispering into the hollow of her throat, "I will." He was kissing her throat now, and his words became an extension, an added dimension, of the intimacy. "Don't worry, sweet Silky. I will."

They were quiet for a time, but Silky remained tensed, her arms and legs holding Wade prisoner within her. A gnawing feeling that something was very wrong was growing, billowing out of control inside her—a feeling that she had put aside and flagrantly ignored when Wade had pressed her down beneath him. But now, reason had returned and she could no longer disregard her foolishness. What could have possessed her? Did she dare excuse her sexual abandon merely because this was a wild, primitive land? Hardly! No, it seemed more likely that this *thing* that had happened between her and Wade had happened because she hadn't been touched by a man for over a year. Simply, and logically put, Wade had just been in the right place at the wrong time!

Another tear slid out of the corner of her eye and was lost in the damp hair at her temple. And what about Rex? What about her plans to get him back? Surely she could still do that, with Wade's promise of silence. The damage was not irreparable.

She let her arms slide away from Wade's back, opening her eyes. Wade would understand. He would help. After all, he probably did this sort of thing all the time. Men did. No doubt he would be relieved that she expected nothing from him—except his discretion. No strings. It had just been a roll in a blanket—a one-time thing.

She grimaced. She'd never been just that to a

man, and it wasn't a pleasant thought. But it was done, and there was no use crying or making excuses about it. She had to put this behind her and go on with her life!

That resolved, she cleared her throat a little weakly. "Wade?"

Chapter Six

*Y*es?" He lifted his head, his smile as gentle as the breeze that ruffled his black curls.

Placing her hands on his shoulders, she whispered weakly, "I'm sorry."

He drew back just slightly. "What?"

Ever so lightly, she pressed against his shoulders. "Could we talk?" Unable to look him directly in the eyes, she followed the broad contour of his shoulder to where it curved downward to become a muscular arm.

"Of course." He lifted himself slowly away, and Silky found herself closing her eyes and expelling a sigh at the wealth of feeling that warmed her core, even in their uncoupling.

With her eyes still closed, she could feel her T-shirt being slipped back down to cover her breasts, cool and glistening with the sheen of their mingled pleasure. With loving fingers, he adjusted her robe about her hips, tying it. Opening her eyes, she looked up into his smile.

"I don't want you to catch cold," he murmured in explanation as he reached for his shorts.

He was being so solicitous, so caring. At least he was going to be a gentleman about this, even if he did consider her nothing but a vacation conquest. She was grateful for that.

When he had his shorts on, she cleared her throat. Sitting up, she felt around for her panties but couldn't find them. Putting aside that problem until later, she smoothed her robe over her lap and sat back on her heels. "Wade, listen to me. I really am sorry." She watched him settle beside her. A curious twist of his brow altered his features.

Lacing her fingers nervously, she went on, "Nobody's to blame here—not really."

"Blame?" He shook his head and chuckled. "What are you talking about, Silky. We just made love, and it was wonderful."

She touched his hand, silencing him. "I thought you'd feel this way. After all, for men, these things are like—playing poker or going bowling."

His brows lifted in surprise. "What things are like going bowling? Silky, you're not making sense."

When he covered her hand with his, she withdrew hers abruptly. This was no time for body contact, not considering what contact with his body had just done to her. She answered rather breathlessly, "Things—you know, brief encounters with women."

"Brief encounters with—?" His lips curved upward in humor. "Silky, you aren't trying to compare what we just did with bowling, are you?"

"Well"—her cheeks went fiery at his intimate tone, and her eyes fluttered away toward the glowing embers for a moment of high embarrassment before returning to his face. "Well . . . I suppose if they were that similar, there would be more bowling alleys."

A completely irresistible laugh rumbled deep in his chest. "Woman, if bowling was anything like loving you, there'd be nothing on the face of the earth but bowling alleys!"

She stiffened at the exhilaration in his tone. He didn't sound like a man who'd just made love to a woman he never intended to touch again. And the fire that had leapt to life in his dark eyes simply did not communicate that he'd lost interest in making love to her—not yet, anyway. On the contrary, Wade looked like a man who had just been given an unexpected, but satisfying, gift.

Good Lord! Could it be that he expected this little *mistake* by the fire to happen again and again during this trip? Did he expect her to allow herself to become involved in a wilderness affair? No! She would have to squelch that notion right now, before it got out of hand.

Lifting her chin, she sat straight, trying to appear regal in her attempt to remain unflinchingly aloof. It wasn't easy, considering the turmoil of her emotions. "Wade," she began gravely. "I was terribly vulnerable—more so than I realized, I guess. This was just as much my fault as yours. I mean, it's been a long time since a man . . ." She came to a floundering halt, feeling her face grow hot. With a great sense of relief, she realized that Wade couldn't see her blush in the darkness.

"I've been alone a long time, that's all. When you kissed me . . ." She let that sentence, too, die away, struggling for something more solid, more logical to blame her loss of control on. Nothing plausible came to her rescue. Crossing her arms self-consciously across the taut tips of her breasts, she tried again, this time edging her words with a firmness she didn't feel. "Try to understand, Wade. My life is completely planned. I'm here on this trip to get my husband back. I'm sure, by now, you've guessed that." Even in her hasty attempt to explain, she stumbled over her words as she saw the hardening in his expression. Clearing her throat spasmodically, she forged ahead. "I—I don't know how this— this thing between us happened, but it won't happen again. Believe me."

With his eyes locked on hers, he slowly pulled one knee up and draped an elbow around it. Nervously, she crossed and then recrossed her arms before her in an unconscious, protective gesture.

He lifted his hand, and began to rub the back of his fist along his chin, a solemn expression creasing his brow. Picking up a pine cone that was lying near the bedroll, he fingered it without interest for a moment before turning away from her and tossing it into the embers. In the waiting silence, Silky listened to the dry pop and crackle of the fragile cone as it burned. When Wade finally spoke, his voice was harsh with an emotion she couldn't quite define. "I believe you when you say you're vulnerable. Hell, Silky, everybody's vulnerable." When he turned back to look at her, his eyes were empty and dark. "Just for the record, your interest in Rex didn't enter my mind. If it had, I wouldn't have—" Mercifully, he didn't put what they were both thinking into words. Changing course, he asked quietly, "So, you want Rex back and your life is planned?" He watched her closely through narrowed eyes as she nodded. "Then do me a favor, Silk. The next time you feel . . . vulnerable"—there was a noticeable pause before he picked up the thread of his sentence— "would you mind picking on somebody else? What we had together was good, Silky, and I'd rather not get addicted to it."

She stilled, and her breathing, if not her heart, stopped as her expression closed in uncertainty. "You make it sound as though *I* seduced *you*."

His lips twisted in a rueful grin as he combed his fingers through tousled hair. "Do I?"

"Yes, you do." For some unfathomable reason, she was unable to continue to look him in the eye, a phenomenon that highly unsettled her.

Dropping her gaze to her lap, she mumbled, "You can't really believe I planned this?"

She felt a finger coax her chin back up, forcing her gaze to meet his. "Yes, I can." Wade's eyes hit hers with the impact of a fist. "Consciously or unconsciously, I think you wanted this to happen. I agree, we were both to blame ultimately. But, now that I know your game plan, I'll be more careful about making rash invitations for you to sit by the fire with me." Heaving himself up, he remarked through a ragged sigh, "I won't try to change the mind of a person who has a cast-iron life strategy. Experience has taught me that much." Catching her by the wrist, he pulled her bodily to her feet. "Maybe you'd better go to bed, Mrs. Overbridge. It's late." He seemed extremely tired, almost disinterested.

Why did she have this nagging sense of loss? Lifting her hand out of his grasp, she tugged her robe up around her shoulders. Straightening it with fluttery, nervous brushes, she belatedly remembered that she didn't have her underwear. "Oh dear." She would have liked to be able to turn and go, but she didn't dare leave a trail of underthings to mark her passing. Her cheeks burned at the very idea of someone finding the lacy briefs in the morning!

"What's wrong?" Wade interrupted her thoughts.

She lowered her eyes, searching the surface of the bedroll desperately. She'd rather not enlist Wade's help in looking for underclothes that moments ago she had allowed him to remove in a fit of passion. Keeping her eyes on the ground, she opened her lips to form a tentative explanation when he interrupted, "Never mind, I see." With a graceful dip of his powerful torso, he scooped up the twisted froth of lace from a shadowed wrinkle in the bedroll and held it out to her. "Here. Take the incriminating evidence and go to bed."

With a wince, she plucked the underwear dangling from his outstretched fingers. Turning away, she stalked into the darkness, knowing full well that tonight her tent would be nothing more than a small, nylon prison where she would get little rest and probably no sleep.

With a bitter sigh, Wade lowered himself back to the bedroll. Hands laced behind his head, he stared up at the twinkling stars, but saw instead Silky's face just the way it tilted up when she talked to him. Her faultless teeth flashed beautiful and white when she smiled in the bright Alaskan sunshine, and her lips . . . His breathing was suddenly shallow, and his heart pounded like a jackhammer gone mad. He'd been struck by her loveliness from the moment he'd first seen her in the hospital. Of course, then, he'd thought she was married. But when she'd joined the bike trip and he had learned that she was single, he had allowed himself to hope that he might be able to build a relationship.

He closed his eyes. Why did he have to fall in love with her? It was now painfully apparent that she only had room in her life for Rex. Wade gritted his teeth. What difference did it make what he thought of Rex? It was Silky's opinion that mattered. Silky . . . his eyes flew open as a cruel flash of memory stabbed at his consciousness. Softly sighing, she was writhing in his embrace, her skin damp and warm beneath his touch. Muttering a curse, his hand jerked angrily up to cover his eyes in a vain attempt to block the moonlit vision of this woman who had so effortlessly, so damnably unintentionally, toppled the barricades he'd built around his heart.

It was ironic that Silky would be the one woman who would assume their coming together tonight was nothing to him but an unthinking flash-fire of passion, when in reality it had meant so much more to him than that. For a year now, he had made sure that any relationships he had begun with women were strictly without emotional involvement. But here was a woman who, in unisex hospital greens, with one brave little speech on behalf of an injured police officer, had sent his tightly controlled emotions scrambling.

"Damn!" he groaned, turning restlessly to his stomach. Sleep never came for Wade, and when the bikers wheeled quietly into camp much later he had done a lot more tossing and turning. But he had also made one tough decision.

No matter how much he wanted it to be, Silky's love life was none of his business. So with a strength of will that he wasn't sure he could sustain, he promised himself that he would honor her decision to mend her broken marriage. And, he would—and this was the intolerable part—he would try to convince himself that making love to her had *not* been the best thing that had ever happened to him. That piece of self-delusion was probably impossible, but no more so than trying to convince someone whom she should, or shouldn't, love.

"Silky?" Wade was whispering her name. Why? She turned over, trying to block his memory from her mind; trying to squeeze the vision of his dark, supple body from her dreams. She wasn't sure how many hours had gone by, but so far, every one of them had been a failure in that regard. The vision of Wade lounging naked beside her had burned into her deepest unconscious thoughts as surely as the road grit burned into her eyes when she was cycling. She only wished that his memory could be as easily removed with a good splash of cold water in the face.

"Silky." Wade's unmistakable masculine whisper intruded into her murky, half-awake world again, this time more insistently. Her eyelids fluttered open and she could see with some regret that it was morning.

"Hmmmm?" Turning onto her back, she stretched.

"Good. You're awake."

Lifting her chin, she raised moss-colored eyes to the kneeling shadow that darkened the zippered entrance of her tent. What did Wade think he was doing? Irritation charged up her spine and she scrambled to her knees, crouching before the door. "Go away! Everyone's asleep!" It was a stern whisper.

She heard his derisive snort. "Fine. If you can keep your voice down, we won't wake everybody else. It's just you I want to talk to."

"Please go away, Wade. It's too early for corrective criticism."

There was a long pause before he suggested tiredly, "Let's call a truce, Silk. Something happened last night that could cause trouble. I thought I'd better tell you first so that maybe we could do something about it."

"You're not going to tell me you're pregnant, are you?" The remark was purposely flippant. She didn't want him to think that the episode by the fire meant anything at all to her. Unfortunately, however, it wasn't quite so easy for Silky to convince herself. The restless night she'd just spent told her that much. Even so, she was determined to put the rash mistake on a back shelf of her mind and try to forget it.

He was unzipping the tent flap. "No, I'm not, are you?"

"Go away!" she snapped.

"Listen, Silk, you've got to come with me and see something. I want you to know I had nothing to do with it. I'm afraid, after last night, you'll think I did it out of spite."

"Did what?"

He had the flap unzipped now. When their eyes met, he didn't smile, but his expression was so earnest, she felt a surge of compassion—or something equally tender—in the pit of her stomach.

He took her hand. "Will you come with me?"

Curiosity grasped her as securely as he did and she was unable to resist. Crawling out of the flap, she mumbled, "Okay. Where is this monumental problem?"

"By the bikes." He did not release her hand as they strode briskly toward the colorful cluster of two-wheelers chained beneath a stand of blue spruce. Silky's mood softened a small measure as she breathed in the fresh morning air and watched the sparkle of dew on the spiky needles.

She grimaced and hopped on one foot. "Ouch!"

Wade halted immediately. "What did you step on?"

"Pine cone." She pushed her night-tousled hair back over her shoulder as she examined the unbroken skin. "I forgot my slippers."

He knelt to examine the foot she had lifted, but before he could touch it, she put it down, discouraging his examination.

"Let me look at it, Silky."

"No, thanks. It's okay." Straightening, she nodded for them to continue. "Let's get this over with."

He looked down at her, his exhale clearly audible over the crunching of his shod feet. "If somebody sees us, they couldn't think we're going to do anything worse than we've already done."

She pulled out of his grasp, whispering urgently, "Must you mention last night? Couldn't you be a gentleman and talk about the weather —or something?

When they reached the bikes, he pointed to the far side. "There. Can you see it?"

Her throat went dry. She was afraid to look, fearing what she might see. But, as they carefully picked their way beneath the branches and around the bicycles, she allowed herself to focus on what Wade was talking about. "Why, it's Rex's bike, and it's . . ." The sentence trailed off as her eyes grew wide. "Wade, it's been—"

"Disassembled." He finished for her. "Beautiful job."

Silky shot a pointed look up at him as he reached up to pick a pine needle from a branch and lay the blunt end between his lips. As she watched, she noticed that his mouth was twitching with barely concealed humor.

"Wade." She gasped. "You didn't."

He shook his head. "No, but I figured you'd think I did." The pine needle shifted from one corner of his mouth to the other. "Do you really think I would be so petty as to take your rejection last night—however belated—out on him?" His hand tightened on her wrist briefly. Releasing her hand, he asked again with some effort, "Do you really believe I would do this?"

Dropping her eyes to Rex's bike as it lay there, so neatly, all parts arranged generally where they would go if the bike were just resting on its side, she bit her lower lip. It didn't seem like

something Wade would do. More like—"Annie?"
She breathed the word before she was even
conscious of her own turn of mind.

"Annie?" Wade repeated doubtfully.

She turned toward him. "Oh, Wade, you don't
think it really was Annie, do you? Rex'll have
her hide if she did this."

A slow smile kindled in his ebony eyes. "Well."
His quick nod denoted satisfaction. "Does that
question mean I'm off the list of suspects?"

She smiled in spite of herself. "Yes, you're off.
I can't really picture you sneaking around taking apart a man's bicycle just because a
woman"—she swallowed nervously at her unin-
tended reminder of what had happened last
night—"chooses him over you."

He lifted a sardonic brow. "This is where I'm
supposed to bring up the weather, isn't it?" Then
with a grin that was very nearly genuine, he
went on, "You're right. I wouldn't take a rival's
bike apart, but I might write the person who did
it into my will." His speculative gaze tangled
with hers. She could feel his vital presence in
the shadowed shelter beneath the pine boughs
as he asked more seriously, "We're still friends,
then?"

There was something in the intensity of his
tone that surprised her. They both fell silent.
Wade was waiting for her answer, and strangely
enough, so was she. Friends? Could she be
Wade's friend? Not long ago they had been
strangers, then acquaintances—however antag-
onistic—then,   heaven   knew   how,   lovers.

Friends? Was that possible? After last night it was very possible that the only route open to them was either to be friends or enemies, and Silky couldn't see Wade as her enemy. She dipped her eyes and forced a mantle of nonchalance. "Maybe—maybe we could be friends, Wade. I'll think about it."

She felt his warm hand squeeze hers. "Good." By the tone of his voice she could tell he was smiling. "Okay, potential friend, let's go tell Rex."

She jerked her eyes up to stare into his. "Tell Rex what?" All sorts of firelit acrobatics scurried through her mind.

The horror in her face must have been easy to read, because Wade was shaking his head. "About the bike. I would never talk to Rex about . . . the weather."

Feeling guilty and silly, she murmured, "The bike—of course. I—I really wish he didn't have to know, though."

"There, you see? We agree on something. Think what a team we'd make if we became friends." Taking the pine needle from the corner of his mouth, he tossed it away. "I'd have put Rex's bike back together myself, but it's an expensive piece of equipment and I figure he'd want to be in on it."

They were standing beside a bike that Silky recognized to be Wade's. He was unconsciously running a hand along its handlebars, gently, almost lovingly. She became mesmerized by his movements, remembering how those same, long fingers had stroked her skin not so many hours before, bringing her body to a trembling pitch she preferred to forget.

"Silky?"

She blinked, unaware that she had lost the thread of his conversation. "What?"

"Where did you go?" He was watching her curiously.

Shifting her weight, she mumbled apologetically, "I'm sorry, Wade. What were you saying?"

He shrugged. "Just that it's too bad we have to wake Rex, since they didn't get in until nearly four."

"Four? How do you know that?"

"I didn't sleep very well." He shifted his gaze to some distant point over her shoulder, and she could see a slight tightening at the corners of his mouth. "Guess I finally fell asleep or I'd have probably heard the culprit." He checked his watch. "It's nine-thirty. We won't get off today until around noon, so that should give us time to get the bike together." He put a coaxing hand to the small of her back. "That is, *if* our bike-razer left all the parts." He chuckled, drawing her attention sharply. "If Annie did this, she's got more grit than even I gave her credit for."

Silky groaned. "And less brains. Please promise me you won't mention her name to Rex."

His light touch at her back mildly guided her through the bikes. "I wouldn't do that to Annie. I think I'm in love with the woman."

Silky sniffed a small, reluctant laugh, feeling

a strange mixture of relief and concern. "So much for the pain of rejection."

She couldn't judge his reaction, being slightly ahead of him, but she could feel his eyes on her as they picked their way through the low pine branches.

She could still feel his gaze on her profile as they headed toward Rex's tent. He said nothing, so she remained silent too, trying to shift her thoughts to Rex and how they would be able to quietly stanch his anger when he was told that his costly bicycle was in pieces. She pressed her lips together to keep them from twitching into a smile. No matter how resourceful a prank it had been, Rex's poor scattered bike was no laughing matter!

A short distance from Rex's tent, Wade whispered, "I'll tell him. You go get the first aid kit. This could get messy."

She shot an apprehensive glance over her shoulder and was relieved to see his smile. Immediately, she lost her battle to keep a straight face and grinned up at him. "Thanks, Wade. But I think I'd better tell him." Running a slightly shaky hand through her hair, she added with forced confidence, "He probably won't throttle me."

"Probably?" He touched her forehead and smoothed back a strand of hair that she had missed. "You're mighty cute when you're fearless. You sure you want to handle this alone? I could stay around."

She shook her head. "I'm sure."

His wink was encouraging. "Okay, but take a piece of advice from an old cop, and tie his hands behind his back before you tell him. When he hears that he has a jigsaw puzzle for transportation he's liable to pounce first and send flowers later."

She screwed up her face in exaggerated pain. "Thanks, I needed that!"

He flashed her a beautiful, teasing grin. "What are potential friends for? I'll get my tools and meet you two at the bike."

Silky shook her head and chuckled in spite of herself as she watched him saunter away, his uneven gait as self-assured as it was disturbingly virile.

Rex took the news pretty well if you consider national disasters and world wars ho-hum trivia.

"*Damnhertohell!*" he snarled, opening his bleary eyes fully for the first time as Silky's news finally penetrated.

She ducked her head out of the tent as he sat up. There didn't appear to be room in the tent for both Rex's anger and her head, too.

"Who *her*, Rex?" she squeaked. "You can't know the person was a 'her.' And please," she pleaded in an urgent whisper, "keep your voice down. Do you want everybody awake? Wade's gone for his tools. We can get this taken care of without any fuss."

"*Fuss!*" On his hands and knees, Rex poked

his scowling face out of the tent, further distorting his expression when he squinted at the brightness of the sun. "Dammit! I want a fuss! I *want* everybody up! I want everybody to witness *Loonie* Toone's execution! I will personally wring her scrawny neck."

Silky shushed him with a finger to her lips. "Rex—" She moved her hand to his arm. "Come on. Think. Annie wouldn't do that!" She hoped she sounded more convinced than she felt. "Besides, whoever did do it won't get any satisfaction out of it if you can laugh it off. Don't you see that?"

Rex was thoughtful for a moment. Crawling the rest of the way out of his tent, he stood up. Silky sat tense, watching. Clad only in a pair of red, terry knit shorts, she was again struck by Rex's fine, lean frame and by how snugly the shorts fit over his slender hips.

He was frowning. "You say Wade told you about it?"

She slid her eyes to his. They were narrowed speculatively as though he were trying to get inside her mind. She felt a guilty lump block her throat and she could only nod.

"Why you and not me?"

She was going to have to lie. There was no help for it. "Uh—he hated to wake you with such bad news since you got in so late. He planned to fix it himself, but because it was an expensive bike, he decided to ask my opinion. I thought you should be told."

Rex nodded, his expression solemn. He apparently accepted her explanation. Relaxing a bit, Silky allowed herself a long, inaudible exhale.

"It all sounds legitimate, but I wouldn't be surprised if Wade wasn't in on this with Annie. They're pretty chummy—though why anybody would want to be chummy with Annie is a mystery to me."

Silky stood up, brushing grass and dirt from shaky knees. "I'm sure Wade didn't do it, Rex."

"What makes you so sure?" he snapped.

"I—I" She couldn't tell him *why* she was sure. She certainly couldn't say that Wade had made love to her; that she'd rejected him and that he'd done his best to assure her that he hadn't taken Rex's bicycle apart out of spite and she believed him. With so much that she couldn't tell Rex staring her in the face she grasped for a straw. "I just don't think a police officer would resort to such a thing, that's all."

Rex's expression softened. "You're probably right." Lifting an arm, he draped it across her shoulders. "Always sweet, always forgiving Silky." He sighed, squeezing her to him. Somehow the intimacy of the move made her feel terrible, having just lied to him to save herself.

"Silky—" he said, patting her arm. "I'm sorry. I shouldn't be taking my anger out on you. Forgive me?" He granted her a dimpled smile.

"There's nothing to forgive, Rex." She reached up and covered the hand on her shoulder with her own. "Let's go. Wade's waiting."

He nodded. "Okay, lady, we'll do it your

way—I won't give Annie the satisfaction of seeing me miffed."

She raised her brows at his mild choice of words. *Miffed* would not have been hers. He was still talking. "Keep your ears and eyes open and let me know if you hear anything. Somebody—be it a he or a she—is going to pay the piper for that little trick. Mark my words."

Chapter Seven

Silky pulled off the gravel road onto a grassy alpine meadow sixty miles east of Fairbanks. An emerald pond dotted with blossoming water lilies lay twenty feet from the road beneath the shade of a semicircle of diamondleaf willows. A few feet beyond the pond, the trees thickened and became as varied as the Alaskan wilderness would allow, with Sitka spruce, pine and several more species of willow drawing a curtain before the countryside beyond.

Some of the more industrious members of the pack were erecting tents. Two orange, a yellow and a fire-engine red one were sprawled across the colorful flora, in varying stages of construction.

Other, less-driven, members of Sag had their shoes and socks off, and were dangling their feet in the pond. That looked like a good idea to Silky, and she rolled her bike toward the water. Thigh-high fireweed, the fuchsia heads dipping and bowing in the breeze, was thick beside the road, making her trek toward the pond no easy matter, but the vision of cool water lapping at tired feet drove her forward.

"Hey, everybody!" Silky turned toward the tenor voice as Leonard Huff hurried out of the dense wall of trees. He pointed back into the woods that hugged the banks of the Chena River. "Wade's found a hot spring back here. Who's in favor of a warm dip?"

There was an instant, almost reverent silence, as all activity stopped. Then Beth slowly stood up, dropping a stake and allowing her tent to billow out and then settle in a red heap at her feet. "Warm?" she breathed. "A *warm* bath?" It came out in a comical mixture of a sigh and squeal as everybody came to life and began scrambling in their panniers for swimsuits and soap.

Today's ride had been easy-paced purposely, since most of the pack had spent the night at the Midnight Sun Celebration baseball game, which, they had been happy to report, the Gold Panners had won handily. Now everyone, even Silky—she realized with some relief—had energy to spare. A warm swim would be a luxurious treat after more than a week of cold dips in streams or outdoor showers. Hurriedly Silky rolled her bike to where the others were chained, and dug out her suit.

"Come on, Silk." She didn't have to turn around to know Annie's high-pitched command.

"Coming, Mother," she joked, taking off her safety helmet and circling the strap over her handlebars. "Where do we change?"

Annie cracked out a short laugh. "Bushes, kiddo. Where's your sense of adventure?"

Silky turned to face her friend. "You're asking a woman who has spent seven days and six nights in the Alaskan wilderness where her sense of adventure is?" Brows raised with mock arrogance, she quipped, "In your hat, Ms. Toone. Lead me to those bushes."

Annie chuckled dryly. "Put a few miles under her belt and she turns into Wonder Woman. Last night's rest sure must have done you a lot of good." With a wave that looked as though it could lead a cavalry charge, Annie motioned them forward. "There's some thick scrub by the hot spring to change in. I'll be darned if that Wade Banning didn't pull this little miracle out of *his* hat. He's really some kind of guy, isn't he?"

Silky didn't answer; an odd lump blocked her throat. She only nodded. It looked as though Wade and Annie were beginning a mutual admiration society of two.

"What's wrong, kid?"

Silky blinked toward her friend, coming to a halt before a low branch that led into the thicket. "Nothing. I'm fine. Why?"

"Hmmm." Annie scratched her freckled nose.

"You'd better tell your face, then. You look like you've just mislaid your last friend."

Mislaid, yet! Annie sure could pick her words! But Wade wasn't the subject Silky intended to broach. Not now, not ever! "Don't be silly," Silky countered, injecting a heartiness into her voice that she didn't feel.

"Come to think of it, you've been acting—goosey all day." Annie was not to be deterred, it seemed.

"Me?" Silky stalled. She'd avoided saying anything about the bike incident this morning, hoping that someone would say or do something that would prove the culprit wasn't Annie. That hadn't happened, and visions of Annie studiously dissecting Rex's bicycle kept cropping up in Silky's mind all day . . . almost as much as the vivid, unwanted memories of her unfortunate—she swallowed—allegiance with Wade.

She stepped over the branch into the thicket with a sigh. "Annie?" Casting a furtive glance around, she whispered, "After you got back from the game last night, did you do anything . . . incautious?"

"Incautious? Jeez! Now there's a great word." She screwed up her freckles in apparent confusion. "Like what?"

"Anything?" Silky coaxed weakly, not knowing quite how to bring the bicycle subject up.

"Hey, love, I never kiss and tell, not even to you."

Silky shook her head grimly. "Don't kid, Annie. I'm serious."

Annie shrugged off her T-shirt. "Seriously? Okay, I was bushed, beat and too tired to pucker. Exactly one and a half minutes after we got back, I was unconscious. Why?"

Not wanting Annie to see the doubt in her eyes, Silky pulled her T-shirt over her head, mumbling, "Oh, no reason." Struggling out of her shorts she asked with feigned nonchalance, "How did you and Rex get along at the game?"

Annie's lips went up at the corners. "Oh, you know. The usual. He glared at me. I glared at him. During the seventh-inning stretch, he sat in my cola."

Silky slid a narrow glance toward her friend's smirking profile as Annie concluded, "That was the highlight of the game, if you ask me."

Pulling on her suit, Silky asked, "Oh Annie, can't you ever leave him be?"

Tying her two-piece at the back, Annie asked blankly, "And take the sun from my sky? Never! You ready to hit the beach?"

Hiking the navy polka dot one-piece over her breasts and tying it behind her neck, Silky nodded. "I guess. Let's go." She knew nothing more about the bike incident, but she knew that Annie was definitely the number-one suspect. What was worse, Annie would be tickled pink to know it!

The mineral spring, Silky discovered, was a nice size, nearly as large as an average high-school pool. Some ancient volcanic thrust had left a jutting of rock at one end, making a natural shelf for sunning. Beneath the surface, another slab of rock formed a shallow area about waist deep, extending fifteen feet out into the pool. Beyond the shelf the water was much deeper.

An avid swimmer, Silky took advantage of the warmth and freedom of the deepest part of the pool. Floating on her back, she watched as an impromptu game of water baseball took shape. A beach ball had magically appeared. Silky smiled, wondering who had come prepared for the absurd eventuality that they might need a beach ball in the wild Alaskan interior!

A whoop went up from the team at bat, if you could call clubbing a beach ball with both fists a bat. Silky glanced toward the game as the oldest man on the trip, fifty-three-year-old George Martin, lumbered awkwardly toward his attractive brunette niece, Riva Healy, who was playing first base. The base itself had been improvised from a plastic garbage bag, filled with air and knotted at its opened end. Then it had been tied loosely with string about the baseman's waist.

George collided playfully with Riva as Wade tossed the ball from second. Silky reflected on Annie's rather colorfully put opinion concerning George and Riva's true relationship. She'd suggested in no uncertain terms that, "Riva is George's niece like I'm Paul Newman's baby sister! Who do they think they're fooling, anyway —out here making hay while the midnight sun shines!"

Several minutes later, a plunk near her face and a sprinkle of water in her eyes announced that someone had hit a home run.

"Silky, throw it back, will you?" Rex called.

"*No!* No you don't," Annie shouted. "Wade gets to score on that one."

"I know that!" Rex snapped back. "I just want the ball. Do you mind?"

Wade had rounded third and swam past Ice, who was playing catcher. He pushed himself onto the rock ledge as Annie plopped down. "Where's Dan, Wade?" she asked. Without waiting for an answer, she cupped her hands about her mouth, calling, "Danny-boy, you're up!"

Wade's laugh, rich and deep, echoed out across the choppy water. "I think it might be better if we don't look for him, Annie. Beth is missing, too."

"There goes half our team!" Annie thrust her arms wide in a gesture of helplessness, exaggerating the loss.

"Two-fifths," Wade corrected. "Randy, you go next."

Silky found herself intrigued by the glinting ripple of Wade's muscles as he brushed his dark hair away from his face. She hadn't spent any time with him today, that is not since she, Rex and Wade had put Rex's bicycle together. It hadn't been a hard chore but, for Silky at least, it had been an extremely uncomfortable hour.

With Rex's arm flung across her shoulders, he and Silky had strolled to where Wade waited beside the disassembled bike. A flash of something Silky couldn't quite read had exploded in Wade's eyes when he had looked up to see them walking toward him so casually connected. That look—like a meteor burning out in the earth's atmosphere—had bothered her all day, and she'd fretted about what it might have meant. But then his eyes had narrowed immediately, resolve hardening his lips. At least it had seemed so in that all-too-brief glimpse. A blink of an eye later, the odd, stony expression had been replaced with bland pleasantness.

Bland pleasantness. That had been Wade's attitude toward her the remainder of the day. Any time he had come within a few feet of her, he'd presented a good-mannered smile and a few polite, but reserved, words before going on his way. It was true that he was behaving exactly as she'd wanted, as she'd asked, but it wasn't making her happy. This new Wade just wasn't the real Wade, not the exasperatingly inquisitive but charismatic person she'd grown to know. Somehow, the necessity of having their relationship move in this direction saddened her.

Riva squealed as Wade struggled through hip-deep water toward first base. They'd gone through the batting order as she'd daydreamed. Holding out her arms, Riva encircled his waist, giggling. "Oh no you don't, Wade. I've got you!" Her musical titter was gay and a bit coquettish, Silky mused darkly as she watched Wade disengage himself from the young woman with a chuckle.

Annie flung herself off the rock ledge. "Oh for

pity sake, Riva. You can't attack a runner like that without the ball! Try to remember what game we're playing!"

"Shut up, Toone! I wouldn't talk *games* if I were you."

Annie, chin jutted for a fight, pivoted toward Rex. Hazel eyes flashing dangerously, she charged. "What do you mean by that, Overbridge?"

Silky tensed for the inevitable confrontation, but apparently Rex changed his mind and waved her off. Pulling the string that secured third base to him over his head, he muttered to no one in particular, "Listen, I'm through. You all do what you want." Turning away, he pushed off the bottom and began swimming out toward Silky with smooth, powerful strokes. She watched as he approached, admiring his graceful form. Rex had always been a fine athlete.

"Hey, Sil." He came up beside her, his voice lowered in a confidential whisper. "I want to talk to you privately. Come with me." He cocked his silver-tipped head, glistening with droplets of water, toward a thicket on the far side of the pool. Silky's throat tightened with anticipation. At last! Rex was going to tell her he was sorry, that he'd made a mistake by leaving her for another woman.

She smiled tentatively, feeling unexpectedly shy. "Why . . . of course, Rex."

He took the lead, climbing out ahead of her and extending his hand. "I think we can have a little privacy while the children are playing."

Smiling coolly, he helped her from the warm water. Her skin was instantly chilled by the cooler air, and she hugged herself, shivering.

Rex noticed her move and laid an arm across her shoulders as he led her into the dense foliage. "It is a little cold when you first get out, but it's still nearly eighty degrees out here. You'll be okay in a few minutes."

They walked a few yards into the trees, where a large outcropping of granite jutted vertically twelve feet into the air, giving them a natural barrier from prying eyes. Leading her into the deep shadow, he pulled her against him with an urgency that almost collapsed her lungs.

Dazed, she could only listen as he muttered intently against her ear, "I've been trying to get you alone for days. If you only knew how I've wanted to hold you like this." He pulled her closer, moving his hands over the damp back of her suit. "You've been incredible Sil, not holding a grudge about Paula. I appreciate that."

Silky rested her hands at his rib cage. Lifting her head, she gazed at his face, waiting for him to go on.

Brushing his lips across her forehead, he murmured, "You look fabulous, honey." A hand slid up her back to the tie at her neck, and to Silky's astonishment, he tugged the strings loose.

Her intake of breath was lost in the sound of his groan. "Ohhh, honey. Let's just say the seven-year itch came a little early for me. . . ." His hand was sliding down and forward, beneath her arm. She knew his objective was her breast, and she felt a disconcerting surge of dismay, even alarm. Pushing away, she clamped her hands protectively over the bodice of her suit, fumbling for the ties. Lips opened, she stared at him, but could not grasp a coherent thought in the ricocheting jumble of emotions colliding in her mind. Feeling lightheaded, she clamped her lips tightly and merely stared.

He was staring too, but his expression was not one of shock, as hers was. Paradoxically, his face held a guileless look of total innocence, a complete lack of understanding for her rejection of his advances. He put out a hand, touching her bare shoulder. "Silky? What is it?" The other hand went out, but she pulled farther away, stepping back into the cold, rough surface of the stone barrier.

"Rex! You can't—we can't—" She swallowed spasmodically. Were things no different at all? Didn't he realize her pride was badly bruised and needed salving, that he had an apology to make? She braced herself mentally. "Rex, aren't you s—sorry?" With her heart in her throat, she watched as his brows beetled. Then a wry grin split his face.

"Is that all? You want me to ask your forgiveness for my sins? You want me to know purgatory before paradise?" He raised a sardonic brow, taking a step forward. With one finger, he lightly teased the skin at the edge of her bodice where it stretched across the swell of one breast. "Okay, Sil. I'll play. I guess you deserve that much." The one finger became four, and they slid unbidden up to the base of her throat where his thumb, resting at the hollow there, began a delicate stroking.

Without Silky's conscious realization, Rex had moved very close again. His breath warmed her cheek as he whispered huskily, "I apologize, Silvia." His other hand circled her back. "I was wrong." The hand at her throat moved up, tipping her chin. Pressing his mouth to hers, he whispered against her lips, "I've learned my lesson. Love me, Sil. Prove to me that I'm forgiven." With a dogged persistence, he tugged at her bathing suit tie again as his lips took hers in a torrid expression of his desire.

Her heart thudded hard against his chest, but it wasn't the trip-hammer palpitation of happy expectancy. It was panic, sheer, desperate panic. Rex was holding her. He'd apologized. He wanted nothing more than to love her. Still she was uneasy. What had he said? *Prove to me that I am forgiven?* Prove to *him*? There was something very wrong, very twisted, in his reasoning. Why must she do the proving? He needed to prove his loyalty and devotion to her! So far, all he had proven was his desire—his physical need, and that was such a cheap, easy thing to prove. Where was the substance, the lasting value in animal need? There was none. He'd found that out with Paula. And she'd seen it even more recently in Wade and, reluctantly, she had to admit, in herself.

Squeezing her eyes shut at the image of Wade, his arms and legs wrapped about her, she reacted more forcefully than she had meant to, surprising herself. *"No!* Rex!" One hand pushing furiously against his chest, she clutched at her bathing suit with the other. "Rex—don't!" Her voice was breathless and tremulous.

He moaned, "Oh, baby," and reached for her again, obviously not believing she was earnest.

Determined to be taken seriously, she slid out from under his arms, backing away from him. Fumbling with her bathing suit, she said hoarsely, "I'm not ready for this. It—it's too soon. You left me for someone else and now you say you want me back. But you aren't willing to do any *work* to get me."

"Work?" He frowned. "What the hell kind of work, Silky?"

Distractedly, she shook her head. Jerking a hand through the wet strands of her hair, she heaved a long sigh. "Work, Rex—*you* prove you want me back. *You* prove you love me!"

"Hell, woman, I was damn well prepared to do just that a minute ago!"

She choked out a half-hysterical laugh. "That's not proof of love, Rex, that's just sex!"

He lifted his square jaw, eyeing her narrowly from beneath long, silvery lashes. "Sex? Why, Silvia Kay Overbridge, I've never heard you talk that way before." Placing his hands on his hips, he shook his head. "I assure you, I'm not just after sex. I love you."

"And Paula? Do you love her, too?"

He ground his teeth. "Can we leave her out of this? That's over. I told you I was sorry."

She turned away, mumbling wearily, "This isn't a school prank, Rex. It's our lives. Just saying you're sorry isn't going to fix everything!"

"Apparently, if you have your way, our lives will be pretty platonic."

She whirled back. "Rex, don't you see? If you want my physical love, you have to earn it. You've got to want me back badly enough to work at it. I—I don't trust you anymore. I want to, but I don't. You'll have to convince me to trust you again."

He gave her a level glance. "What do you want me to do, spit on every woman I meet? Would that do it?"

Her gaze dropped to the ground. His face had become too blurry to see. Desperately she blinked back a shimmer of tears. "All I want is to be—be loved enough to be a man's *only* woman." She spoke so softly that her plea was no more than a thread of sound. "I want to be very, very sure that I am, Rex. I'm willing to work at our relationship—"

He snorted sarcastically. "You couldn't prove that by me! From here, it looks like I do all the work for very little pay."

Hurt-filled eyes snagged his. "Well, *you* did all the cheating!" She'd never allowed herself to use that word before when referring to, or even thinking about, what Rex had done. Often she'd called his affair a "mistake," or referred to his philandering with the catchy little phrase, "big men have big egos," or "boys will be boys." Never before had she used that one, totally descriptive, totally correct, horribly ugly word. Now tears formed in her eyes and slid down her cheeks, feeling cold against her fiery face.

Their eyes battled silently for a moment before he relented slightly, one corner of his mouth quirking upward. "You can really hit a guy where it hurts, kid." He dropped his head in a single, heavy nod. "Well, now that I know the rules, I guess it's my serve, right?" He pursed his lips, waiting.

She wiped at her cheek, smiling weakly. "I guess." The almost completely doused hope she had carefully carried around in her heart for the past year leaped into flame with his answering smile. He lifted a fist to her chin, clipping it lightly as he taunted, "Where's that agreeable little girl who married me?"

With her smile gone awry, she lifted her chin. "She grew into the woman who divorced you."

The sound of angry voices silenced them and they turned simultaneously toward the mineral spring. Silky recognized the first voice to be Ice's. He was clearly quite exasperated, and she felt a pang of guilt. With all that had happened since yesterday afternoon, she'd completely forgotten about his request for her to get closer to Randy.

"Mega-stupidity, kid! Where'd you get those?"

"Aaaah, Ice. Don't get hyper. It ain't no sin."

The cracking and crunching of underbrush being trampled grew louder as they lumbered over bushes and through low branches. Preoccupied with their argument, they were doing a decidedly poor job of trailblazing.

"It *ain't,* huh!" Ice mocked. "And just who says so? Didn't I tell you smoking'll kill you before your time?"

Just then, Ice saw Silky and Rex for the first time. Circling his hand about the back of Randy's neck, he halted them both. "Oooops, sorry for the intrusion, people. We were just brainstorming for the antismoking spots I'll be running this fall on WROK. Weren't we, kid?"

His expression pinched, Randy raised his eyes toward the couple as he answered, "I guess so. . . ."

Silky's heart went out to the boy for his embarrassment, not only for being lectured for having cigarettes, but for having his punishment witnessed. It didn't take much insight to see that it was a tough combination for the boy to take. At least, to Ice's credit, he had tried to make light of the situation for the boy's sake.

"Well," Rex said with a meaningful glance at Ice and Randy, "I guess this party's over. I'd love to stay and chat, but I'm on the fire detail. I'll go on back to camp and get my trusty little axe."

"Hey, man," Ice said. "I'd better get on back too. I've got a tent that needs pitching."

With hardly a pause, Ice looked at Silky, remarking with apparent unconcern, "Silky? Could you show Randy here some of the basics in swimming? He swims like a steel guitar, and I do mean *steel!*" His world-worn eyes were asking much more than his lips. They were pleading for her to go through with her end of the bargain, but he didn't have to beg. Silky knew that there was no escape for her. If Randy was going to get lousy news on this trip, she would do her damnedest to be sure that he didn't get it like a punch between the eyes!

Winking down at his bleak little face, she smiled. "Sure. I used to teach swimming for the Red Cross back in Kansas, Randy. What do you say we hit the water?"

"Guess so." His slouched shoulders lifted and fell as he skeptically scanned her face. "I seen how good you float."

"Thanks. Floating's a snap. It's all a matter of filling your lungs with air."

"Yeah?" With eyes narrowed in doubt, he muttered, "I'll sink. You got better lungs 'n me."

Rex choked back a laugh while Ice loudly cleared his throat. "Your lungs are fine, kid, so long as you keep that damned smoke out of them. Now you go on with Silky."

Silky tugged at Randy's wrist as the two men walked away. While they picked their way back toward the mineral spring, Randy said nothing, and she couldn't tell from his deadpan expression if he was happy or irritated about being thrust into her care.

"Randy, let's go over to the shallow end to start."

As they neared the edge of the hot spring, her eyes skimmed over the others still present. They were no longer playing ball. Riva was quietly

sunning beside George. Wade, Annie and Leonard were sitting on the ledge above the water.
Annie was swirling her feet in the water and
speaking with animated gestures. As usual, she
was entertaining her audience. Silky just hoped
the subject of her dialogue was not Silvia Kay
Overbridge.

Wade's eyes caught hers as she jumped into
the waist-high water. His ebony eyes were no
longer laughing. They were deadly serious.
Turning abruptly away from the haunting stare,
Silky felt a pang of guilt. He knew that she had
been in Rex's arms.

A tap on her shoulder startled her. "What—?"
"I said, we gonna float or not?" From that
frowning little face, it sounded more like a dare
than a question. Did the poor child expect her to
desert him too?

Trying to shake off the strange feeling of mis-
conduct that Wade's look had caused, she distractedly patted a damp cowlick into place at the
crown of Randy's head. "Sure—sure we are,
Randy." Hoping her smile didn't look as fraudu-
lent as it felt, she bent her knees, dropping down
until the water lapped at her chin. "First, we
relax."

Inwardly, she had an insane urge to laugh out
loud. What a luxury it would be to relax. In her
present state of mental turmoil it was an impossible task. Last night with Wade had been the
undoing of her sexual integrity. Just now, she
had been through a messy scene with the man
she loved. Finally, Ice had burdened her with

the bitter responsibility of breaking Randy's heart.

"Okay, I'm relaxed." Randy broke into her thoughts as he matched her position in the water.

"I'm happy for you."

"Huh?"

"Nothing, honey." She smiled sadly. "You're doing just fine."

Chapter Eight

$\mathcal{D}$inner long over, Sag Pack was quiet, and the long Alaskan day had surrendered to darkness. Yet, even in the peaceful quiet, Silky couldn't sleep. Restless, she crawled soundlessly out of her tent, not sure what she expected to do, only knowing that it would do her no good to toss and turn, trying to sleep.

She stood and looked up at the sky, gasping in surprise. It was pulsating with the gossamer light patterns of the aurora borealis, glowing green and blue, then orange and red, in lively disregard for what should have been the brief north-country night.

She smiled up at the celebrating heavens, glad now that she hadn't been able to sleep. Though she'd seen the northern lights before, the spectacle seemed to take on a singular importance out here in this vast wilderness. If she missed a single, lovely undulation, would the beauty of the lights be lost forever because it had gone unseen by any man's eyes? For the first time, Silky was consciously glad that she had made this lunatic-fringe trip with her crazy friend. Maybe there was something to be said for madness after all!

Strangely buoyed by that thought, she struck off toward the hot spring. She had always had a secret urge to swim in the nude. This secluded place in the Alaskan interior, under the majesty of the aurora borealis, seemed like a perfect place to make a memory, to create a mental souvenir of her trip.

Standing on the jutting rock above the warm pool, she pulled off her robe and slipped off her T-shirt and underwear. A splash accompanied her as she slipped into the pool. The water caressed and lightly massaged her skin as she skimmed along with graceful, silent strokes. Executing a perfect surface dive, she circled beneath the surface and came up to retrace her path toward the shallow end. Reaching the rock shelf that formed the shallow, she stood, clearing the water from her face as she walked toward the rock ledge where her clothes were neatly folded.

Looking up, she froze, but the water continued to move and sparkle about her, teasing and patting at her belly and hips. A masculine shape loomed above her on the shore. The broad silhouette was backlit by the undulating fire in the sky, and she could see ebony curls flutter in the night breeze. Only when Silky felt the rush of air cool her naked torso did she remember her state of undress and belatedly cover her glistening breasts, lowering herself into the water. "What are you doing here?" There was no real shock in her whisper, only a kind of dismayed surprise.

"I—" he began rather haltingly. "Annie woke me. She saw you wander off and was worried about you. I thought I'd better check."

Silky's jaw worked in embarrassed agitation. "Where is Annie?"

He gazed thoughtfully at her for a moment. "Back in bed, I guess."

She sniffed. "She must have been worried sick. Well, you may go back and report that I'm just fine."

"Just fine?" He shook his head slowly, but with certainty. "From what I've seen, you're damn perfect." Uninvited, he sat down, patting the rock as though it were a sofa cushion. "Since neither of us can sleep, what do you say we sit and talk?"

She opened her lips in amazement at his casual suggestion. "I'm not getting out. Surely you noticed I—I'm not—"

"I noticed." He favored her with an unexpectedly sensuous smile. "With a little coaxing on your part, you might be able to convince me to join you."

At the strangled sound of a moan in her throat, his smile faded slightly, but in spite of that, he chuckled dryly. "That's good enough. I'd love to."

"Wade!" She choked as he started to shrug off his shorts.

He stopped, his thumbs hooked at the waist-band. Glancing down at her with a completely believable look of innocence on his face, he asked mildly, "Yes?"

She held out her hand. "I—I'll come out. Toss me my robe."

He seemed to consider her offer for a moment before his mouth softened at one corner. "You sure? I wouldn't mind a swim."

Stifling another groan, she stiffened her arm, lifting it higher. "Please, Wade. Give me my robe." He grinned briefly before bending to scoop up her wrap. With carefree enthusiasm, he tossed the terry projectile the few feet over the water. She caught it easily, but not without raising a bare inch too high out of the water. Wrapping the robe hurriedly about herself, she eyed Wade as though he were a grizzly bear and she, the only morsel of food left in the forest. It was not comforting to note that his eyes glittered with laughter.

The robe was soaked from her waist down, and the absorbent fabric was heavy, clinging to her hips as she pulled herself from the water. Stepping a bit away, she turned her back on Wade and wadded the tail of the robe, squeezing out as much excess water as she could.

As she worked, Wade remarked casually, "The

northern lights are unbelievable, aren't they? I've never been this far north before. They're even more spectacular up here than in Anchorage." His voice, now at waist level, told her that he had settled back down on the rock.

When she turned to face him, he smiled up at her, nodding an invitation for her to sit. "I hear they're really something at the North Pole," she said, tugging her robe securely.

"Me, too," he agreed as she joined him on the rock. "That's a sight we'll have to see."

The word *we* startled her. "I don't think Sag Pack's route goes quite that far north."

Dismissing the idea with a laugh, he observed, "I think your friendship with Annie is rubbing off on you. You're starting to sound more like her."

Silky shrugged. "I'll take that as a compliment if you don't mind. Annie's got a lot of spunk. I admire that about her."

He grunted derisively. "Don't worry about that, you're getting there." There was a trace of false heartiness in his smile. "At least I've run across a pretty wide streak recently." He paused, looking directly at her.

Unable to bear the directness of his look, she lowered her gaze to her lap. She didn't want to be reminded of last night. Quietly she sidestepped. "Nice weather we've been having."

The noise he made wasn't quite a chuckle, at least it didn't hold the humor of one. "Okay . . . back to Annie. I guess, with two ex-husbands, she's had to form a little crust, but basically she's a caring person." Absently, he picked up a pebble and tossed it into the water. Silky watched as it skipped across the surface in a series of slight plunks before sliding silently beneath the surface.

"You like her a lot?" Silky asked carefully.

"Sure. You're lucky to have such a loyal friend."

She shrugged. Mirroring his earlier move, she picked up a pebble and tossed it the same way he had. But it thunked heavily and dropped beneath the surface a foot from where they sat. "Annie's loyalty can be a double-edged sword," she gritted, gesturing toward him. "You for instance. I don't need her smothering me with armed bodyguards."

His mouth crooked. "I'm not armed."

She felt a quiver rush up her spine that had little to do with the night breeze. He had said absolutely nothing to warrant the flush that warmed her skin and set an odd, pulsating heat deep within her. But she couldn't hold back the errant thought that the man *was* definitely armed; his weapon, a devastating, all-consuming one.

Shifting uncomfortably, she dropped her eyes. "Uh—I meant that figuratively. "You know— you're a cop, and all." Finally, highly irritated with herself, she set an edge to her words. "I'm surprised that you figured Annie out so quickly. It took me a year to find out she had a heart."

Trying for a cool, blasé façade, she said casually, "I thought cops were more physical—"

"More physical?" he interrupted, appearing vaguely amused.

She lifted her chin. "If I'd been allowed to finish, I would have said, 'more physical than mental.' You know, assume guilt and leave the proof of innocence to the courts."

"Oh." He gazed at her steadily through half-lowered lids, but the amused glitter in his eyes was gone. "Look, Silky. I don't plan to fit into your file drawer of stereotypes. Try, just once, to find the real person"—he laid his hand, fingers spread, on his bare chest—"the one *inside*. You might be surprised at what you find." He started to stand, but Silky took his hand, halting him before she was even aware that she didn't want him to leave.

She lifted apologetic eyes to his set face. "I'm sorry, Wade. I didn't mean to offend you." Wanting to make amends for her unintentional affront, she coaxed, "If you want me to see the person . . . inside you, then stay and tell me about him. Have you been married?" She blanched at her question. Where in heaven's name had it come from? A question she'd never considered asking, a question that was none of her business, had slipped out unbidden!

He slid a curious glance toward her as he settled back down, extending his legs and leaning back on his hands. "Married? No." His expression turned thoughtful, and his glance wandered out over the dark water. Silky had the feeling that he wasn't seeing the water, but another woman's face. "I had a fiancée."

"Fiancée?" she repeated, breathily. A tenseness stole over her muscles. Attempting not to show it, she drew her knees up and rested her chin on them.

"Maureen and I were to have been married a week after the accident. Of course it had to be postponed. By the time I was well enough, I told her that I wanted to leave Detroit and move out here."

She couldn't help herself; suddenly very interested, she sat erect.

"She—" He paused, clearing his throat as he looked back toward her. "To make a long, dull story short, she made it clear that she loved Detroit more than she loved me. She wouldn't leave her friends and family to—'be shut up in an igloo eating blubber.' That's a cleaned-up version of her opinion of Alaska." He sat forward, dusting off his hands. "Maybe I should have said ex-fiancée."

"I—I'm sorry," she fumbled. "You must have been unhappy."

"I was for a while. But I realized our love had never been strong enough to last. If it had, I'd have stayed in Detroit to be with her, or she'd have come to Alaska. Both of us are better off."

Silky pushed a strand of hair behind her ear, but she didn't speak. She could only stare at his handsome face. Somehow it came as a shock to her that any woman worth her hormones would

be so stupid as not to follow this man to the very
ends of the earth—which of course Alaska was!
Or at least it had seemed that way when Rex had
mentioned the prospect of moving here shortly
before they were married. She felt her tensed
features soften, understanding something of
Maureen's dilemma. Still, that didn't excuse
her! Through thinned lips she exhaled. "Yes, I
think *you* are definitely better off."

Wade appeared vaguely amused by the play of
expressions that had crossed her face. "Thanks.
I don't regret what happened. The experience
has just made me careful about women." The
perceptive glance he leveled on her had a bait-
ing quality about it. He said nothing for a long
moment before remarking quietly, "Right now,
I'm just working on making friends. You for
instance—I'd like to be your friend, and I'm
willing to work for it." He tilted his head, watching her closely. "Maybe even as hard as you're
working to get Rex back. I wonder who has the
tougher job."

Silky tugged at the lapel of her robe, suddenly
oddly self-conscious. "Making a friend isn't so
tough, Wade."

He shook his head. "You're thinking of an
acquaintance. I want to be your friend—
someone you can talk to—someone who can talk
to you."

"We're talking, aren't we?"

He rubbed his fist across his mouth. "No.
We're conversing."

"Well, what's *talking*, then?" She wasn't sure

she should have asked that question. But now
that it was asked, she steeled herself for whatever was to come.

He eyed her evenly. Wade was a man prepared
for the challenge. He nodded. "All right. Why do
you want Rex back after what he did to you?"

She winced as the unexpected question hit
her, like the slap of a storm-tossed pine bough,
right between the eyes. "What?" She shot back
the defensive question fiercely. "And just what
is wrong with wanting to make a success of my
marriage?"

"What marriage?" He said it so quietly that
she wasn't positive he had actually said anything. She blinked wide, hurt eyes at him as he
went on, "Look, if it's just a matter of feeling like
you've failed in some way, that's ridicu—"

"You want to make me your friend and I want
to get Rex back," she sputtered tremulously.
"No question, Lieutenant, you have the tougher
job!" She jumped up, gathering her T-shirt and
underwear as she pivoted to escape.

He grabbed her arm with a strength which
only hinted at the physical part of his job that
she had seen him exhibit at the hospital. "Just
be sure," he whispered through gritted teeth,
"be very sure, Silky, that getting Rex back isn't
just a matter of pride with you. Don't get caught
up with images of what is right. They don't
always reflect what is real." She jerked at his
hold but couldn't pull free. Nostrils flaring, he
growled under his breath, "Not all marriages
are good ones, Silky. And not all divorces are

mistakes." He let her go so abruptly that she almost fell before regaining solid footing and rushing off into the trees.

How appropriate for clouds to have set in over the pack. For days they had doggedly followed Sag, and now they looked threatening. Thunder, off in the distance, helped make their decision to pitch camp early.

It was just after four o'clock, somewhere between Woodchopper and Eagle. Trees as dense as fur on a husky's back hugged the mighty Yukon River as it flowed majestically some distance north of their camp.

"Silky." Rex ambled over and put a gloved hand on her handlebars. "Since you're on dinner detail, why not let me put your tent up for you?" He ran a finger across her knuckles. "I'll put it next to mine, by the fire. Okay?" His wink was conspiratorial. "Is this more like what you want?"

She squinted up at his confident grin and tried to appear stern. But his dashing boldness was too much for her to resist. With a reluctant smile, she unfastened her safety helmet. "It's a start. And, thanks—I'd appreciate it."

As she chained her bike to a tree, Annie trudged over, her eyes animated with a sparkling mixture of concern and delight. "Say, Rex . . ."

He swiveled at the sound of her voice, stiffening. "Can't you see I'm talking to Silky? I'd rather not be disturbed right now."

Annie shrugged in a comical exaggeration of helplessness. "I'm on your side, dollface, but I think you're gonna be disturbed whether you want to or not."

He raised his eyes to the sky and sighed expansively. "Well, what is it?"

Annie scratched her ear, her eyes drifting disinterestedly off toward the gravel road. "Nothing really—your tent's catching on fire, is all." She'd said it so casually that neither Rex nor Silky believed their ears at first. After a motionless second, both jaws dropped and Rex shouted, "My *what's* on fire!"

Annie smirked, shaking her head. "Naw, just your tent." She gestured over her shoulder. "I told you not to set up so close to the fire with this wind."

He exploded, grabbing her shoulders. "Why you little—*you did this!*"

Silky jumped into the fray, pulling one of Rex's arms loose and slipping in front of Annie. "Rex"—she tugged at the front of his nylon shirt—"come on. We need to see about your tent!"

The urgent tremble in her warning brought him back to sanity. "The tent!" He dashed off toward the fire.

Silky followed, but not before she gave a chilling look to her friend. The deep green glitter in her eyes clearly communicated that she thought Annie's sense of humor would put her in traction one day. Unruffled, Annie only grinned.

The tent was scorched and dirty, but whole.

Quick action by Wade and Leonard, scooping damp earth onto the flames, had smothered it before any real damage had been done. Rex knelt to examine the nylon as Leonard, wiping his hands on a towel, assured, "It's quite sound."

Nodding in agreement, Rex came up off of one knee. "Looks okay. Thanks." He held out a hand toward Leonard. "Say, if you have any clout with that redheaded arsonist, give her a good kick in the pants for this, will you. I'd kill her."

Leonard's big moustache twitched with his frown. "You've eluded me there, Overbridge."

Rex flipped a finger at the nylon, raising a cloud of dust. "To put it bluntly, Huff, Annie set my tent on fire to be spiteful."

Leonard's mild eyes widened. "Say now, friend. I'd have to argue that—"

"Yes, Rex," Wade interjected, scratching a cheek darkened with a day's growth of beard. "I saw what happened. The wind blew some burning pine needles near the tent. Annie had nothing to do with it."

Rex looked doubtful. "No? You sure?"

Leonard nodded. Wade raised a brow as though his word was not ordinarily questioned.

"Rex, setting tents on fire is kid's stuff. When I get you, it'll be deadly—but it'll have class. I promise." Annie clapped him on the back. "I'll tell you what. I'll help you move this filthy hovel and then you can help me scrape carrots for dinner. That way you can keep an eye on me." Clapping him one more time, a little harder than might have been considered comradely, she motioned to Silky, who had lagged behind. "And you, lovey, go gather some fireweed. We need a salad. Take your time and just get the tender shoots."

Silky shook her head in faint amusement. Nodding, she turned away. "One nature salad coming up."

For fifteen minutes, she meandered, picking the fuchsia-tipped weed along with several other varieties of edible plants that she'd become familiar with during the trip. There was something very satisfying about gathering food from the wild. But for the occasional rustle of leaves, and the distant tremble of thunder, she felt as though she were walking in a fragrant painting . . . except, of course, the bear cub was moving.

Bear cub! She became a ramrod with eyes, watching as the baby bear romped in the tall grasses beside the path. Like a carefree child, it tumbled and bounced up, only to tumble again in its zigzagging route toward her. After the initial shock, Silky relaxed, smiling. Lifting her bouquet, she waved it at the cub, calling softly, "Hello, baby." Cooing as though she were talking to a human infant, she called again, "You're a cute little thing."

The cub stopped and stared, twenty-odd feet away, looking every bit as startled by her presence there as she had been by his. She laughed. "Don't be afraid of me."

A loud rustle in the shadows of the dense trees

beyond the small clearing announced another presence. Silky squinted into the deep shadow, but could see nothing. All she was sure of was an apprehensive tingle at the base of her neck. She would have given anything to know that the roar that vibrated through her was only the bawl of thunder. She swallowed spasmodically, frozen to the spot.

In the next instant, she was shoved off the path, beyond the line of trees, and thrown unceremoniously on her face into the mud. She tried to lift her head, but she was restricted by a heavy weight as a hoarse whisper ordered, "Lie still and keep quiet!"

She had only been able to turn her face slightly to the side, but at least she could breathe even if she couldn't see. "Wha—"

A hand clapped over her mouth, and she could feel the cool ooze press against her lips. Deciding that she didn't care to eat any more of the stuff than necessary, she kept her mouth shut.

The bashing sound grew nearer and then stopped like the mighty silence of death. She could feel her heart beating like a berserk woodpecker in its attempt to move the blood that had frozen in her veins.

Oh, why didn't something happen! A sudden rustle above, in the direction of the path, grabbed her complete attention. A low snarl followed closely and she squeezed her eyes shut. She'd always heard that at times like this, a person was supposed to see her life flash before her, but all she could see was the horrible flash of angry bear—over and over.

The rustling grew more distant, and the snarling stopped. Was the bear going away? Was she actually going to remain alive? And if she was, would she ever be able to stand erect again?

Slowly the hand lifted from her mouth as the hushed voice gritted, "If you keep living with such abandon, you're going to end up abandoning living."

Silky spit mud. Recognizing Wade's voice with a mixture of amazement and regret, she exhaled heavily. "Off!"

His low chuckle rumbled through her. "What about the grizzly?"

"Tell him to get off, too."

"Her."

"What?" Silky turned her head further, eyeing him suspiciously as best she could with her face caked with mud.

"It was a her—a mama bear protecting her young."

Silky's weighted lungs expelled a disgruntled moan. "Almost done in by a cliché."

He chuckled again. "Maybe so, but I must admit it was a damn sight more exciting than most clichés you run into."

She tried to elbow him in the ribs. "Off."

"Sure?" he asked easily, her effort to dislodge him failing miserably.

"Wade, you're crushing me."

"Maybe if you turn over?" The suggestive

overtones in his question were as plain as the mud on her face.

"Get off of me, Wade Banning!" she ordered through clenched jaws.

He made no move to obey. "Is that all the thanks I get for saving your life?"

She wriggled, then grimaced at the slimy feeling of the wet dirt against her body. She could only speak with difficulty, considering the press on her lungs. "Thanks . . . now—get off."

"Ahhh, that's better." He rolled away. Sitting up in the goo, he put his hands on her arm and helped her rise. "I was afraid you'd make a flowery speech and embarrass us both."

Ignoring him, she plucked at her muddy T-shirt. Looking down, she could see that her nipples were taut beneath the once-pink nylon fabric. Her mud-covered face became a mixed blessing, when she realized that her fiery blush of mortification was hidden beneath it. Wrinkling her nose, she could feel the thick stuff pull at the skin on her cheeks. "I can't believe this happened."

"I'm looking at it, and I can't believe it." He reached up and wiped some mud off her face. Fighting a smile, he reprimanded softly, "Don't you remember what I told you about walking along wooded paths out here?"

She lifted a grimy chin. "Beware of men who throw you into mud?"

He smiled slightly. "I'm glad to see that you can face a grizzly and not lose your sense of humor. No. I meant, if you must use the paths, make some kind of noise—sing—talk to yourself."

She sniffed derisively, "Why? Don't bears attack crazy people?" Without waiting for his answer, she pushed herself up to stand, almost falling back into his lap in the slippery mud. "Oh!"

He reached out and caught her by the hips. "Very funny." He kept one hand on her hip as he stood. "But it's better to look a little crazy than be a bear's leftovers."

She jutted her chin, glaring at him, but her stern frown melted as she scanned his mud-streaked face. Black curls that fell across his forehead looked as though they had been dipped in chocolate. His hands and forearms were encrusted with mud, and his shorts and legs were caked. He looked every bit as much the victim as she did, and for the first time it hit her that Wade had really risked his life to save her! Shaking her head incredulously at the new thought, she smiled up at him. "You know? You don't look so good, Lieutenant. I wonder if Sir Galahad got that dirty. Maybe you just need a little more practice."

He crossed his arms at his chest. "No, thanks. I figure if you live through a grizzly attack, you're as perfect as you need to get."

There was a little smudge of dirt on his cheek, and as they smiled at each other, she found it totally impossible not to reach up and brush

away the mark. "Thank you, Wade," she murmured.

His gentle expression mirrored hers, but he
said nothing. He seemed to be waiting for her to
go on. Lowering her hand self-consciously, she
mumbled, "Why are you here, anyway?"

"I came . . ."—pausing, he flexed his jaw, un-
crossing and then recrossing his arms—"to apologize for the other night." Silky could sense the
effort that this declaration was taking.

"Dammit, Silky. I know your personal life isn't
my business. I—I'm sorry I butted in." He expelled a breath in barely controlled anger, running a muddy hand through his hair. "I give you
my word I'll stay out from now on." Raising a
finely arched brow, he asked, "OK?"

Her heart went out to him. Lowering her gaze
thoughtfully to his hand clenched at his side,
she answered carefully, "To be honest, Wade,
that fight may have saved my life today." She
lifted her eyes to meet his again, and when her
gaze met his, the contact was surprisingly soft.
Breathing a little shallowly, she finished, "An
apology isn't necessary."

He smiled, nodding obligingly. "All right,
then. I have just one more question." Swinging
his broad shoulders down, he plucked the
muddy, broken clump of fireweed from its
mucky grave. Knowing that he had been forgiv-
en, his dark eyes twinkled with fun as he asked,
"Shall we toss the salad?"

A laugh gurgled up from her throat. "I've

never seen one more in need." Touching one limp stalk, she suggested, "You do the honors."

Flipping the muddy greenery over his shoulder, he grinned. "Done. Now if we work together, we'll have a salad gathered in no time."

"Maybe later." She shook her head. "I've got to get out of these clothes before they harden on me."

His look was vivid and penetrating as he touched the side of her cheek with his thumb, smoothing away a fleck of dirt. "May I help?"

Something in his tone made her eyes flutter uneasily away and her mud-caked skin feel flushed. Nervously, she cleared her throat of an odd obstruction. Lifting tentative eyes, she regarded him with wary determination. "You know the answer to that, Wade."

He pursed his lips, and she thought she could see a tensing in his jaw before he nodded. "Yeah. I may be a cop, but I'm not a dumb cop."

She lifted her chin. "Now who's talking stereotypes?"

He chuckled. "Okay, okay." Changing the subject, he cocked his head toward the trees away from the path. "The Yukon River is just over there, if you want to clean up."

"Really!" she exclaimed in an excited breath. Craning her neck, she squinted into the thick line of trees. She could see nothing, but she thought she could barely hear the rush of water. "Thanks, Wade." Single-mindedly, she headed off past him in the direction he'd indicated.

He took her wrist, swinging her around on the

slippery ground. "Hold up a second. You don't think I'm going to let you traipse off alone again, do you?"

She frowned up at him. "Why not?"

"Because you're a far cry from Daniel Boone, for one reason. Besides, I need to clean up, too."

"You?" she squeaked. You can't come with me. I'm going to wash my clothes."

He shrugged in easy acceptance. "So am I. Don't worry. I'll stay a gentlemanly distance away."

She raised doubtful brows. "Just how many miles, exactly, are in 'a gentlemanly distance'?"

His laughter rumbled like deep thunder. "I'll stay too far away to grab, and as a bonus, I'll turn my back."

"You're all heart, Lieutenant," she grumbled darkly.

With a sidelong expression of amusement, he put a casual arm lightly across her shoulders and propelled her over the grassy rise. There, like magic, glistened the Yukon River as it churned and rushed around a wide bend.

Silky stepped out from under his arm. "You go on downstream." She arched her arm high, pointing as though she were taking in a good deal of the earth's surface. "Stop when you get to Brazil."

"On the other hand," he asked mildly, "can *I* trust *you* not to peek?" With her answering groan, he grinned and turned away, walking some twenty feet down the gravel shore.

As Silky peeled off her crusty clothes behind a

low, water-hugging bush, a soft rain began to fall, gentling her spirits with its cool cleansing. She waded out into water that was waist deep, making sure to keep her back toward Wade, and began scrubbing the mud out of her top and shorts.

A sledgehammer crack lit up the sky and its angry rumble made her stiffen. Her first panicked thought was that the bear had returned. But, remembering the lightning, logic returned, and she realized that it was just the approaching storm, now much closer.

Another blinding crack ignited just above her head as lightning tore through the dark clouds like a punishing cat-o'-nine-tails.

"Silky!" Wade shouted over earsplitting thunder as the gentle rain gave way to a pelting downpour. Jerking her head toward him, she dropped to her shoulders in the water.

"Silky—get out! It's dangerous to be in water when there's lightning." He was waist deep, motioning broadly for her to go to shore. Even if the thunder had been too loud for her to hear him, he was making it very clear what he wanted her to do.

With her lips pressed stubbornly together, she shook her head. "No! I want to put on my clothes first."

A flash of anger illuminated his deep scowl as he dove into the water. *He was coming to get her!* Gasping, she sank until her chin was in the water. She held up a fist, shaking her shorts at him defiantly. "Wade, don't you da—" A few powerful strokes, even into the forceful current, had her in his arms. "Waaaaade!" she screamed angrily as he carried her toward shore. The charged sky caught, for a silver instant, the wild, natural potency of their bodies in a glistening silhouette as he carried her, flailing and fighting, out of the river.

Chapter Nine

The rain battered and blew them, and more than once Wade nearly lost his footing on the slippery river rocks. Instinctively Silky stopped struggling, throwing her arms about his shoulders, burying her face against his throat.

Regaining his balance, Wade moved forward again. Silky couldn't tell when he left the water and she didn't care. With the unforgiving rain spiking her skin, something inside her gave up the fight. Wade had already beaten her, and she was afraid that the rainstorm might ultimately defeat them both.

"Silky—" he gasped. She felt cool softness at her back as he laid her down. "I think we'll be okay here."

Opening her eyes, she lifted her head from his shoulder. He had carried her into a mossy thicket, protected from much of the wind and rain. Looking beyond his shoulder past the protective arch of low branches, she could see the hard rain pelt the land and river alike with equal brutality.

Nature's voice was deafening. The steady roar of the river was joined with jolting regularity by the rockslide rumble of thunder and the harsh dazzle of lightning, while the wind howled eerily in the branches above them. Stray drops of rain filtered into the thicket, dropping tentatively to the carpet of moss like the timid tapping of a lost child's finger.

Wade knelt down beside her. "It's beautiful, isn't it?" His observation drew her eyes from the rain-soaked landscape as he smoothed a wet strand of hair from her cheek. "Makes you wonder why people live in cities, doesn't it? Life is so intense, so full of power out here."

The staccato flashes of lightning outside their natural shelter drew her eyes for an instant, but just as quickly she shifted her gaze back to the unsettling beauty of his animated face. Long, dark lashes were spangled with water, and his eyes glittered darkly with a strange, masculine sorcery. She was still holding his shoulders lightly as he knelt there, looking steadily down at her. She knew she should have been angry—only a moment ago she had been furious. But all of her irritation slid away, like drops of rain. Slowly, she opened her lips. "Wade—I—"

Thunder cracked around them and lightning turned the world outside their shelter stark white. It was terrible and wonderful—like the tumultuous struggle of a brave new world—nature's birth cries. And Silky felt a part of that new birth: part river, part earth, part sky and part storm; elements of it all—she and Wade—small but vital parts of the swirling maelstrom of nature. Without reason, she felt an unexpected surge of hunger to know the fullest force of another storm, one as undeniable and fierce as only the joining of flesh to flesh can ignite. Her body ran hot. Her veins were a wild network of charged electricity, while her heart beat in frenzied concert with the pulsating world beyond their refuge.

"Wade . . ." It was a throaty, desperate sigh. She didn't have to say anything more. The plea shimmered in her eyes, as she communicated her need in a language that was older than the spoken word. Before her eyes, his concerned expression changed to a brief flash of surprise and then to a gentle softening that was not quite a smile. As he lowered his lips to hers, she breathed, "I want to be a part of the storm, Wade—part of you . . ."

Thunder applauded their kiss with the clap of a billion unseen hands as Wade lowered her to the yielding moss. His groan was one of male hunger, not protest.

Even with her eyes closed, she could see the lightning flash and hear the melodic moan of the wind. The mossy den smelled faintly of musk, but her conscious mind held none of these sensations as dearly as it did Wade's touch. His large, warm hands traveled over the slick, curving surfaces of her body like a thorough explorer.

Reluctantly, he lifted his lips from hers as he smoothed the hair away from one ear. Lowering his cheek to hers, he gently tugged at the lobe with his teeth. A wave of heightened feeling danced like leaves in a high wind along her body, setting fire to her core. Her moan of pleasure mingled with the wind's deep cry, and she opened herself fully to his searching touch.

She shuddered, reaching out for him, trying to speak. Her words were broken by a sigh as his expert fingers sent a wave of raw need through her. With shaky hands, she pushed against his shoulder until he was lying on his back. "Wade— let me ride the storm."

He said nothing, but watched her silently as she slid over him, taking him inside. Gasping at the delicious pleasure of his entry, she curled her fingers in the mat of wiry hair at his chest.

Tilting her face to the green, swaying roof that protected them, she let out a shuddering sigh and raised her hands to his shoulders. His name took flight on the wind, as he pulled her forward to nuzzle and suckle her breasts. She reveled in the feeling as his tongue teased them. Pulling his face close, she let a soft laugh, deep in her throat, go free. She was mother earth, and he, the raging storm that nourished her and gave her life.

Slowly she began to move. Wade's hands slid down to her hips as he joined her, aiding her. Lifting her head, her eyes closed, she allowed that part of her which was wholly primeval to move her through each thunderously exciting clash of their bodies, each breathtaking flash of feeling, until at last, with Wade gripping her thighs, she raised her face to the sky. Her cry of fulfillment echoed out over the maelstrom.

Wade gently touched a quivering breast as he slid his hands around to her back, and pulled her trembling body down to cover his. Smoothing her hair away, he kissed her cheek. She could feel the shudder of his muscles as he held her tightly to him. Still imprisoned within her, he lay holding her.

At first she was still, watching his profile. Then, with one hand, she began to stroke the hairs that curled sleek and shiny as black patent leather against his tanned face. She licked the droplets of rain from his forehead, and then moved down, first closing one of his eyes with a gentle kiss on the lid, and then the other. She didn't know what wanton had taken over her body, and she didn't care. Lifting her head, she delighted in his expression as he opened his eyes again to gaze up at her. It was extraordinary, a combination of wonder and something very close to adoration. Loosening his hold he began to unleash new feelings of excitement within her as his fingers lightly massaged her back and hips.

"Why do you think this happened, Silky?" he whispered hoarsely, his eyes intent, questioning.

She started at the unexpected question and tried to rise, but he anticipated it, pressing her face to his throat. She could feel his pulse coursing against her lips.

"No—" he cautioned softly. "Think about it before you say anything." His other hand continued to feather her back with caressing strokes. "Why do you think we made love again? Considering what you said your feelings were, doesn't it seem odd that you keep falling so easily into my arms?"

She felt sick, and a tremor defied and won out over the stiffening of her lower lip. It wasn't until a whimper betrayed her devastation that Wade released her and she was able to pull herself away, sliding quickly off of him and scrambling to her knees.

Feeling very confused and hating herself for her unexplainable weakness, she sat back on her heels, covering her nakedness as best she could. Eyeing him through a blur of tears, she mumbled distractedly, "What do you want me to admit, Wade—that I'm a weak person, or that you're God's sexual gift to women?"

She grabbed her clothes from where she'd dropped them earlier and began to struggle into them. Wet and clinging, they fought her every inch of the way.

Wade sat up abruptly, touching her cheek. "Listen, Silky! Listen to your—"

She slapped his hand away. "Stay away from me! Maybe I am weak, I don't know—" She jerked her top over her head. "Maybe it was just the storm. You know what they say about storms." With legs as weak as her tremulous voice, she stood.

"Silky, look deeper than that." He reached out for her wrist, but she avoided his touch as though it were a snake's.

"No! There's nothing to see! You and your constant preaching about looking beneath the surface." She pushed a hand through her tangled hair. "It's really very simple. The storm frightened me—and then it excited me. That's all. Don't try to make yourself out to be some sort of macho Adonis. And don't think I'm some weak-kneed, easy—" She choked on a sob. "I—I just made a mistake with you." With a bitter moan, she corrected herself, biting out fiercely, "Two mistakes! But I won't make any more."

"You can't mean that," Wade said levelly, his eyes holding hers relentlessly.

Her legs quivered so badly she wasn't sure that she would be able to support herself. Weakly, but with ironbound determination, she managed, "I mean it, Wade." Her shadowed green eyes narrowed to slits. "Rex was my husband. He will be again." She drew a long, shuddering breath. "I want you to stay away from me. Do you understand? Leave me alone!"

This last came out in a mournful cry as she spun on her heels. She could hear him curse violently under his breath as she dashed out of the shelter. Running blindly along the rocky bank, she was hardly aware that the rain had slackened, but she was very aware that Wade was letting her go, and her relief was strangely subdued.

"The lieutenant fix your ticket out there in the woods?" Annie's sarcastic quip pulled Silky sharply from her gloomy reverie as she narrowly watched Wade glide by. She shot her head around so quickly that her helmet skewed sideways on her head.

"What?"

"Wade Banning. You remember him. The long arm of the law?" Annie cackled evilly, flicking a finger on Silky's askew headgear. "Better tighten your strap or a good wind'll catch it and screw your head off." She lifted her lips in a knowing smirk. "I've been dying to ask. Just what happened between you and Wade out there in the rain the other night?" A devilish twinkle sparkled in her hazel eyes as Silky gasped.

"Oh, you covered yourselves pretty well—for the rest of the folks. But not me! You may have come in from the west, and ten minutes later he straggled in from the north, but—" She lifted a finger for emphasis. "How come he had the salad stuff and you had nothing but a flimsy excuse about falling in the river? How come ever since, you've been looking daggers at him? Jeez, Silk! A person could get killed getting caught in the path of one of your glares. What's the matter, kiddo?"

She watched Silky's pink face intently as she casually squirted water from her bottle into her mouth. Fastening it back on her bike frame, she went on, "It's plain to me that the man's made a pretty big impression, and I have an idea what kind of impression he made." She lifted her lips impishly as the double meaning of her words hit Silky square in the face. "But what I can't figure is why you're so darned mad about it. Most women would give a lot for a romp in the woods with—"

"Leave it alone, will you!" Silky ground out between clenched teeth. Pushing hard on her bike pedal, she left her friend standing by the roadside in the yellow brown dust that her hasty departure stirred up.

Why did Annie have to be so painfully on target? How humiliating that she had guessed. This "romp in the woods with Wade," as Annie had so roguishly described it, was one subject that she would never discuss. She couldn't understand why she had succumbed to him. But no matter what the reason, she wouldn't let it happen again. Annie may have guessed the truth about Wade and her, but she promised herself that she'd never say anything that would make Annie absolutely sure she was right. It wasn't anyone's business. Besides, it would certainly never happen again!

She pedaled at top speed, partly to get away

from Annie and partly to catch up with Randy. How ironic that Ice's distasteful request for her help had actually become her salvation these last few days. Even Rex's deliberate attentiveness had begun to get on her nerves.

Randy Douglas needed a friend and, right now, so did she. She and little Randy were two people drawn together by a mutual need, no strings attached.

She grinned wryly at Randy's skinny shoulders as he pumped determinedly up ahead, his oversized orange helmet bobbing up and down with every move.

"Hey, Randy! Wait up!" she called.

He squinted back over his shoulder and tossed her a tentative half-smile, his version of uninhibited mirth. Slowly, almost imperceptibly, he reduced his speed so that she could catch up. As she passed Ice, he nodded, his mirrored eyes telling her nothing, as usual. But his sad smile was one of unspoken thanks. Silky mused that Ice's behavior toward Randy was odd, considering his continued insistence that he wasn't old enough to handle the responsibility of a boy Randy's age. He seemed like a better-than-average father as far as Silky could see. Sure, the boy made him mad at times, but she thought Ice handled Randy justly.

Whatever else Ice had learned in life, he had learned compassion. He was a man who had walked on feet of clay and learned, from his own mistakes, how to forgive. His flamboyant DJ pose could easily lead a person to believe that he had little substance, but Silky had discovered that what she saw was only a shell. Ice was a gentle person. It surprised her a little to realize that she was growing to like him.

"What's up, doc?" she kidded, as she caught up with Randy. Yesterday, when she'd told him that she'd been an emergency medical technician, he'd shyly admitted that he wanted to be a doctor. She'd told him that he could do whatever he wanted to do with his life. All it took was hard work and determination. Silently, she hoped that life would grant him his chance.

"Nothing." He kept his eyes ahead.

Silky shook her head and grinned—her man of few words. They rode along in comfortable silence for a while with the steady crunch of fine gravel crackling like static beneath their narrow tires. Silky tried very hard to keep her eyes off of the broad shoulders of the man leading the pack.

Angry with herself for her unsettling preoccupation with Wade, she forced her eyes to slide toward Randy again, struggling for a topic of conversation that might take her mind off Wade.

"Did you hear? Annie told me that we're going to camp in an Eskimo village tonight and celebrate the Fourth of July with them tomorrow. How about that?"

He reached up, pulling the short bill of his safety helmet forward. "Yeah? You think they got firecrackers?"

Silky laughed. "I'll bet you a can of soda they do."

"How 'bout a beer?" he queried, his face comically deadpan.

"Cute kid." She reached out in playful reprimand and tapped the brim of his helmet, sliding it lower on his forehead.

He grunted. "I ain't."

Silky watched out of the corner of her eye as the skin behind his freckles flushed a rosy pink. His expression soured as he frowned and slouched forward. Her brows compressed in confusion. What had upset him—that she'd called him "cute," or "kid"?

Shadows were long when word was passed back that they would soon be reaching their destination. Though the weather had been good, for Silky it had been a long, dreary day. She was looking forward to tomorrow's festivities. Maybe a celebration would help take her mind off her troubles. She certainly hoped so!

"No hot dogs for me." Silky pushed open the door of the cheerful new school building and walked out into a stiff breeze. Dodging the whipping American flag and the sky blue Alaskan state flag that were planted proudly on either side of the cement steps, she nudged Annie, challenging, "We want to try the smoked fish, don't we?"

Annie ran both hands through her curls and inhaled deeply. Silky had no doubt about her answer. She'd do or say anything to be different.

Putting a thin arm about their chubby hostess, Genny Chocolate, president of the village corporation, Annie assured, "Hot dogs are for tourists, kiddo." She pursed her lips as though she were about to expound greatness. "Like I always say. When in Rome—eat the smoked fish."

Genny's round face lit up. A vivacious forty-year-old, Genny looked half her age, with short-cropped, blue-black hair and shiny, dark eyes. Genny and several others of the village leaders had been kind enough to take the pack under their collective wing and accompany them throughout the day's festivities. Silky couldn't think of a better way to learn about the natives in her adopted state, and she was determined to learn all that she could.

Genny patted Annie's hand as it rested on her shoulder. "Good girls. I'll let you in on a little secret. It really hurts the elders when outsiders make fun of our traditional foods and the old ways. Your open-mindedness is—"

George pushed open the door with Riva and Wade close behind. Silky, Annie and Genny moved to the bottom of the four cement steps to clear the way. Riva nodded to them. "Hi, ladies. Georgie, Wade and I are going to join Dan and Beth for hot dogs. Want to go with us?"

Annie took her arm from about Genny's shoulders and shook her head. "Naw. Silk wants some smoked fish, and I've got my taste buds all primed for some caribou jerky and a big bowl of Eskimo ice cream."

"Good God!" Riva put a theatrical hand to her throat, making the muffled sound of someone who was about to be very ill. "I heard how they make that ice cream, Ann. It's mainly boiled fish and lard with some sugar and berries mixed in. I'd die before I'd eat that stuff!" She smiled sweetly down at Genny, shrugging back her dark hair. "No offense, of course, Mrs. Chocolate."

Genny's smile was pleasant, but Silky could see a very slight narrowing of her eyes. Genny had not been pleased by Riva's thoughtless remark, yet her answer was gracious. "No offense taken. Many people feel as you do." She put her arms about Silky and Annie's backs. "Now, if you'll excuse us?"

Wade asked, "What are they doing over there, Genny?"

"At the fire?" Genny turned in the direction he had indicated. "Oh, they're burning smoked fish skins. It makes a crispy snack. Would you like to try some?" She smiled inquisitively, almost suspiciously, up at Wade, who was nearly twice her height.

His grin was lopsided and easy. "Nothing ventured . . ." His eyes slid casually to Silky's before he continued, "Nothing gained. Let's go." He stepped away from George and Riva. "I'll see you folks later at the drum dances."

"Oh, great, Wade. Do join us." Annie laughed, reaching around Genny to poke Silky teasingly in the ribs. "Like I always say, there's nothing like a little snack in the woods to brighten a man's day. Right, Silk?"

Silky said nothing, hoping that her stare would convey the message that she'd received Annie's shrouded little innuendo, and that someday she would get her just revenge. She only hoped Wade hadn't realized what Annie had meant! Breaking eye contact, she turned away. But she was uncomfortably aware of Wade's presence at her back. The air crackled around her, and she felt flushed. It was ridiculous, she knew, but that didn't alter the fact that she felt like she was about to be jabbed with a cattle prod. Breathing slowly and deeply, she worked at slowing her heart rate. Why did Wade's presence unbalance her metabolism so? He was like a six-foot flu bug.

While the other three chatted, Silky tried to concentrate on anything else, looking desperately about her. She couldn't pronounce the Eskimo name of the village, but Genny had explained that it meant "Precious Home." With a population of a little over two hundred, this "Precious Home" was a streetless village, dotted with windswept huts and frame houses sitting almost shyly among sawtooth-edged spruce. They had traveled nearly a mile down a deeply rutted dirt road to reach the remote village, but the side trip had been worth it. The natives had taken them in like family, given freely of themselves and their possessions—food, entertainment—all free. These kindhearted people were selflessly giving the biking pack of strangers a Fourth of July that Silky would always remember.

She looked to her left to scan what would have been Main Street, had there been a street. There were only two log buildings there. One was the general store, with a crudely painted sign that read just that. The other was the village community center, used for all town meetings. But the largest and newest building in town was the one they had just left. The schoolhouse, Genny had explained earlier, had been the result of monies provided for long-neglected native villages through the Alaska Native Claims Settlement Act of 1971. Their schoolhouse, with carpeted classrooms and rubber-compound gym floor, was their pride, and the focal point of most of the holiday activities.

She felt a hand on her shoulder. Wade's voice, deep and inquisitive, broke through her thoughts. "Would you like one?" He held a frizzled fish skin toward her. With a reassuring gesture, he added, "It's good." Silky nodded, accepting it with a smile.

"And now"—Genny dusted her hands on her faded jeans—"let's get some cranberry juice to wash it down. And if you're still game, we'll try some ice cream."

They weaved their way in and out of wandering natives and other packers who were eating traditional Eskimo fare or downing hot dogs and pop. Round-faced native children ran barefoot through the noisy throngs, setting off firecrackers and giggling at the surprised reactions of their elders.

"Hey!" Silky turned in unison with her small group to see Ice waving and hurrying toward them. Randy's head was caught in the crook of Ice's arm, and he was being dragged reluctantly along. When Ice reached them, he let the boy go, giving him an affectionate scruffing on the head. "Is this muscle-head something or isn't he? I hope you people didn't miss the head-pull contest!"

Wade chuckled, handing the boy a fish skin. "No, we all saw it. Congratulations, Randy." Scanning the activity around the fire, Randy silently munched on the skin without comment.

Ice crossed his arms in front of him, puffing out his chest. "I swear that kid he beat had him by a good twenty pounds."

"Aw, Ice," Randy mumbled. "He was prob'ly only ten or eleven—just a kid." Plugging his pockets with his hands, he dropped his eyes to the ground, embarrassed by the praise.

"Maybe so, but he was six-two if he was an inch. Besides, you've never done the head pull before." Turning toward the group, he lifted his glasses to his head, reliving the event with uncharacteristic excitement.

"Actually, Randy, the boy you beat was thirteen. You should be very proud." Genny's smile was encouraging. "Are you going to enter any more games?"

Randy shook his head, but didn't look up.

"Are there more?" Ice was interested.

Genny motioned for Randy and Ice to join their group. "After lunch, yes. We still have the seal hop, knee jump, one-foot-high kick and leg wrestling. The boys and girls love the competitions."

"Apparently the parents aren't bored by them either," Wade interjected with a wry look toward Ice.

Genny giggled. "Oh, you're so right. It's our homemade version of the Native Youth Olympics. The games are just a few years old. They were started in hopes that the young people of Alaska won't forget the traditional contests of their forefathers."

Randy looked surprised. "Them kids gotta be tough, I guess," he mumbled.

Silky was first to voice the question as she put a hand to Randy's chin, lifting it. "What do you mean, champ?"

He skewed his mouth to the side and shrugged. "Heck, if they had four fathers—I'm only on my second, but I know it's tough to keep changin' dads."

Silky felt a threatening tingle behind her eyes as tears began to well up. Her throat closed in mortification at this brief glimpse of the boy's raw scars at being abandoned, first by his real father, then his mother and soon . . .

A look of compassion swept across Genny's sweet face. She patted the boy's shoulder. "No, dear, forefathers just means ancestors."

"Oh." Randy blinked at the short woman who stood at exactly his eye level.

Ice's quick movement caught Silky's eye. He lowered his mirrored glasses over his eyes. But before he did, Silky was sure that she had seen them cloud. She gritted her teeth with the reminder that they would be leaving for Whitehorse tomorrow, and it was now only a matter of days before Randy was to be left with a stranger. Soon, she would have to tell him that, and her insides churned with the distasteful reminder.

Wade cleared his throat, drawing Silky's eyes. He seemed to be searching for a more pleasant subject. "I—I heard something about drum dances. What are they?"

"Drum dances?" With a quick nod, Genny directed the group to follow her down a well-trod path. "They'll be tonight. The village boys and girls pantomime traditional Eskimo ways: seal hunting, picking salmonberries, stalking geese—" She cocked her head over her shoulder and lifted her lips in shy humor. "We even have a basketball dance, but it's fairly new."

"Mrs. Chocolate," Randy asked, "when's fireworks?"

"Late, Randy. It'll be long after midnight before it's dark enough. But it'll be worth waiting for." She pointed toward a frame house, freshly painted a light yellow. "Here's Anishia Friendly's place. She makes the ice cream. And I know she always has cranberry juice ready. How about some?"

Silky took a deep breath, steadying herself for

the experience by trying not to think about either fish or lard. "I'm game."

"Me too." From the sound of his voice, Wade had moved up very close behind her, and her skin began to tingle, alerting her metabolism to go haywire again. Oh, why didn't he just go away!

Annie peeped inside the open door. "Anishia Friendly? Eskimo ice cream made under that label can't be bad."

"Are you a glutton, or just a glutton for punishment?" Annie grimaced sympathetically toward Silky's dessert dish after the huge offering of the outdoor celebration dinner. "First, porcupine roast, fish eggs and cooked fiddleheads, and now cranberry-and-whitefish *agutuk*?" She lifted a forkfull of chocolate cake. "Honey, not even the Eskimos are eating only Alaskan dishes. There are limits, you know. Give yourself a break."

Silky pushed the side of her fork into the dessert, shaking her head. "No, Annie. I may never have the chance to taste this food again."

Popping the chocolate cake in her mouth, Annie said sarcastically, "Yeah, I know." She mumbled around the mouthfull of food, "You're no quitter. Okay, Napoleon, it's your Waterloo. Just don't come crawling to me at four o'clock in the morning with an *agutuk*-ache."

Silky chewed the slightly sweet dessert, fairly sure that she wouldn't mind never having it again, but glad, at least, that she'd tried it. She scanned the neatly kept grounds in front of the white-painted school building, where ten of the cafeteria tables had been set up and piled high with all types of Alaskan and more traditionally known American foods.

Villagers and packers alike had filled and refilled their plates and picnicked on blankets or grassy spots beneath the Sitka spruce. The day had been long, but exciting, with the tour of the village and schoolhouse, and the Youth Olympics. Silky shifted, crossing her legs in front of her. Yet to come was the children's presentation of the traditional drum dances in the school auditorium, and then the procession to the bank of the local creek, where the fireworks would be enjoyed in the brief summer night.

She put her plate down on the borrowed quilt, swallowing. Closing her eyes, she frowned at the odd feeling of disquiet in her stomach.

"What is it, Sil?" Rex asked. Sitting across the patchwork blanket from her, he put his plate down and leaned forward.

Annie groaned. "She's sick! I knew it!" Putting a gentle hand on Silky's, she asked, "Didn't I tell you so?"

Rex pulled up on his knees, moving closer to her. "Are you?"

Silky moved her head in a way that wasn't quite a negative shake or a positive nod. "I—I hope not." She ran shaky fingers through the fine blond hair at her temple. "But I think I would like to go to my tent and lie down for a while."

"I'll take you." Annie put a supportive hand to

Silky's elbow and was about to help her up when Rex interrupted.

"No need, Annie. I'll go with her." He quickly stood and bent to help Silky up.

Annie looked at him with narrow suspicion. "We'll both take her."

"I will!" Rex took Silky by the shoulders, drawing her tightly to him. She could feel her stomach churn as she thudded into his side. "You go find Leonard and pester him for a while. Then when you make him sick, you can help him to his tent."

"Hey, you two—why don't you go on and fight. I'll just toddle off to die, okay?" Silky's voice was so weak, it sobered her two overzealous protectors.

"Oh, honey, I'm sorry." Annie was contrite.

Rex didn't relinquish his hold. Pulling her off in the direction of their camp, he said sardonically, "Truer words were never spoken." Flashing a wicked grin over Silky's head toward Annie, he offered gayly, "Say good night, Gracie."

"Rex Overbridge," Annie shouted toward their backs, "I've met a lot of people in my life, but you're not one of them!"

Silky dropped her head; she just didn't feel like refereeing anymore. Rex ignored Annie, much to Silky's relief. He held her tightly with one arm about her shoulders. "How you doing, Sil?"

She shook her head. "I don't know. Maybe if I lie down a while, it'll pass."

He squeezed her shoulders. "I hope so. You'd hate to miss the fireworks."

Silky searched the foliage for the first sign of their camp. She felt clammy and weak, and she was afraid that every step would be the last one her legs would successfully execute.

"Just over there." Rex cocked his silver blond head, and Silky's listless gaze slid to the right.

She sighed heavily. "Thank goodness."

Crawling inside her tent with nothing on her mind but curling up and trying not to be sick, Silky was surprised to find that Rex joined her in her cramped quarters. Raising up on one elbow, she asked weakly, "What are you doing?"

He smiled knowingly. "Joining you." One hand slid down her bare arm to rest on her nylon-clad hip. "Getting to see you alone is one hell of a chore, honey. You're always with that watchdog Annie or that bothersome kid."

Silky looked down at the hand on her hip. His fingers were tickling the fabric. Taking his wrist, she moved his hand away. "Rex, I don't feel very well."

He shook his head. "You'll be fine in a minute. I'll see to that." Lowering his face to hers, Silky was appalled to realize that he was about to kiss her. His hand moved to her stomach this time. She felt like she'd been jabbed with a hot poker.

"Rex!" she moaned, backing into the nylon. "Do you want me to be sick all over you?"

His brows beetled. "Don't be silly, Sil. You aren't going to be sick. Come on, now." He slid a hand up to cup a breast and his brashness made her inhale sharply.

"Rex. My God!" She pushed his hand to the bedroll. "You can't be serious."

"Never more serious, darling." He slid closer to her, lifting his relentless hand up to slide over her waist to her back. "I'm dying for you," he whispered, kissing her jaw and murmuring, "Soon as we get back to Anchorage, let's get married again." His hand had slipped beneath her blouse and toyed with the waistband of her shorts.

Her stomach lurched violently as he pressed his aroused male hardness against her, and she compressed her lips to hold back the rising feeling of nausea in her throat. Beyond the sensation of physical illness, she also became aware of another kind of unease. Something wasn't quite right. What was it? Hadn't Rex just proposed? Of course, he'd picked a terrible time, but he'd asked her to marry him.

His hand at her back became more aggressive, as his fingers moved slowly down over her hip. Only the gauzy lace of her panties separated him from her bare skin.

"No." She pressed her fisted hands against his chest. "Rex, I'm sick. Please leave me alone." Pushing herself up, she slid around him toward the tent entrance.

He grabbed her shoulder. "Hey." His fingers tightened, and she grimaced, craning around to look at him. His features were a mask of anger, and his eyes glittered harshly. "I've put up with a lot from you on this trip. And I've been a good little scout because that's what you wanted." Without relinquishing his grip, he crawled to face her. "But, it's my turn. What's wrong now? I said I'd marry you. What more do you want?"

What more? She stared, her eyes wide. Rex was as devastatingly handsome as ever, with the white blond hair of an angel, and the silver-tipped lashes of a movie idol. He was tall, intelligent, a stylish dresser; he knew the best wines and the best places to eat. But, suddenly, she didn't know what he looked like, what he really was. It was as though she had never laid eyes on him before. Where was the real person in this neat, well-built male shell? Didn't he see that she was ill? Didn't that matter to him at all? Would he never learn to think about another person's feelings? Was he so self-centered that he saw only what he wanted to see?

She was confused. Shaking her head, she whispered with an unsteady rasping in her voice, "What more do I want, Rex? I—I don't know. Something." Looking up unswervingly into his eyes, she ordered quietly, "For now, just take your hand off of me and go."

He challenged, "Are you saying you don't want to marry me?"

She pulled her knees up, hugging herself. "I don't know what I'm saying."

"That's the damned truth!"

Her eyes were riveted on her knees. Without looking up, she knew he had left her alone.

Oddly, her nausea was completely gone. But, in a trade that seemed only fair, considering everything, her head was pounding unmercifully.

For a long time, Silky didn't move, preferring to sit and count the throbs in her head—anything was better than thinking.

Chapter Ten

Wearing slickers as protection from the constant drizzle, they passed into Canada. The days of dismal rain that followed helped disguise the real reason for Silky's black mood from everyone. Everything, from clothes to bedrolls, was damp and dreary, and there had been little talk while packers conserved their energies to battle the mud and rain and cold. Tomorrow they would reach Whitehorse and, so far, Silky hadn't had the strength or the heart to say anything to Randy about being left with his mother's second cousin.

Late that afternoon, the sun had finally come out, and their camp was teaming with activity as, at long last, a hot dinner was being anticipated. Tonight Silky was on cleanup duty, so she was free until later. Maybe now would be the time to talk to Randy—

"Damn you, boy!" Rex bellowed, jerking Randy by the neck of his T-shirt. "Where did you think you were going with my biking shoes?"

Silky's jaw dropped, and she jumped up from the stone where she had been sitting. "Rex, let go of him. For heaven's sake, he's just a child!"

"Hell, Silvia. This child, as you so generously call him, was stealing all three pairs of my biking shoes. What was I supposed to do without them, borrow your sneakers?" He yanked Randy forward and the boy settled in a slouched, but not cowering, stance, looking dourly toward Silky. A crowd had begun to gather.

"What's wrong?" Wade asked quietly.

"Nothing that a good thrashing wouldn't cure." Rex released the boy, and put his fists on his hips. "This kid was stealing my biking shoes." He jerked his head to the small litter of shoes behind them. "I knew all along that he was no good. Now he's proved it."

"Maybe he was just living up to your expectations, Rex," Wade offered mildly. "I don't mean to make excuses for the boy, but this constant rain has made us all a little buggy." With a small nod, he motioned for Randy to come with him. "We'll have a little talk, okay? After all, I do represent the law here." He looked around at the others. "Is that okay?"

There was a vague, disjointed nodding among the numbers. Silky looked around, wondering where Ice was. Almost immediately she had her answer.

"Hey, fellow rockers, what's the gig?" Ice ambled out of the woods with an armful of dead willow branches. "The kid been being a kid again?"

Wade hung a loose arm about the skinny boy's shoulders. "It seems that Randy was making off with Rex's biking shoes. I was just about to ask him why. Would you care to come along?"

Ice nodded reluctantly, dropping the willow branches by the cleared area where the fire was to be built. "Guess I'd better. What's with you, kid? You got a thing for shoes?"

The two men and the boy disappeared into the trees. Silky stood stiff and nervous, watching them go. Still, somehow, she felt that Randy would get a fair hearing, and that relieved her.

"I wonder if Annie didn't pull those pranks, after all? Maybe I'd better apologize to her." Rex had walked up to join Silky, but he was talking to himself.

"Clever boy. I guess you can't always tell brains by appearance." Annie appeared out of nowhere, nodding her red curls obligingly.

"You're mighty quick with the answers, aren't you, Toone," Rex grumbled.

"Not really, big fella. It just seems that way to you." Silky struggled to hide a smile as Annie went on without pausing, "Why don't you get a pair of those irresistible shoes on, barefoot boy, and we can go finish gathering that firewood. It won't be so easy with all this rain we've been having." She took his elbow in a strong grip and turned him away from Silky. Squinting back over her shoulder, she called in a mock whisper, "If we aren't back in an hour, assume we've done each other in and eat cold cuts."

Ten minutes later, Wade, Ice and Randy came back to the camp. Ice went back to getting the fire going, Randy crawled into his tent and Wade resumed setting up his own tent. Silky couldn't stand not knowing what had happened. Laying aside the paperback she'd been pretending to read, she brushed the seat of her shorts and walked over to Wade, whispering conspiratorially, "Well?"

He was on one knee, pushing a metal stake into the soaked ground. Lifting his head, he looked up at her, his expression purposely blank. "Well—what?"

Silky sat down beside him on the grass and leaned forward. They were behind his tent. No one could see them from where they were. Scowling at him, she coaxed urgently, "What happened out there with Randy? Did he tell you why he stole the shoes?"

"He wouldn't come out and say why, but it isn't hard to figure. The kid's jealous of Rex, Silky. He's in love with you."

"Who—" She swallowed. "Rex or—"

"Randy." Wade watched her face for a moment before adding, "I can't say about Rex. Sorry." Silky ran a nervous hand through the fine, blond hair at her temple as Wade went on, "He admitted that he took Rex's bike apart, too."

He pursed his lips. "He didn't mention letting the air out of Rex's tires that first day. If he did that, he must have fallen in love with you when he first laid eyes on you. Poor little guy." He shook his head. "A few more like that, and you'll have your own basketball team."

"What?" She wasn't quite sure she'd heard him right.

He smiled at her, but the pleasant expression didn't quite make it to his eyes. "Nothing." Flipping the stake in the air, he caught it. "I had a feeling about Randy, but—"

She interrupted. "Did you two punish him? I saw him crawl into his tent."

"Ice told him to apologize to Rex."

"Did he say he would?"

Wade laid the spike down, chuckling wryly. "Not only did he say he would, he already has. Rex and Annie make a loud pair of wood gatherers. They weren't hard to find."

Silky sighed, putting a hand to her cheek. "Good." Then, looking back up into Wade's face, she asked, "Then why did he go to his tent?"

"He's humiliated, Silky. The kid needs time alone." He brushed the dirt from his hands, reaching out to touch her shoulder reassuringly. "Don't worry about Randy. He'll get over his crush. Kids do it every day."

Silky chewed on her lower lip. "I'm not worried about that, Wade. I know I'm no femme fatale. It's not that." She exhaled heavily, leaning back dejectedly on her hands. "It's just that this has come at the very worst time."

Wade quirked a brow, leaning closer to her and resting a palm near her thigh. "What do you mean?"

She could feel the radiant heat of his arm near her leg. Feeling awkward at his nearness, she shifted her weight away. Allowing her eyes to drift along his shoulder, she couldn't help but notice how nicely the aqua color of his biking shirt and shorts contrasted with the deep tan of his face. "I—what I mean, Wade, is that Ice plans to leave—" She swallowed with difficulty, as her fingernails dug into the damp earth. "Ice doesn't want Randy—doesn't feel that he can take care of a child Randy's age. He's going to leave Randy with some distant relative in White-horse tomorrow." The story was falling out in a distasteful rush of words. She needed someone else to know, and it seemed that that someone was going to be Wade. "And Wade—he's asked me to be the one to tell Randy he's going to be abandoned again! *Me,* Wade! Don't you see how much worse it's going to be on Randy—on both of us—now that you've told me how Randy feels about me?" Distractedly, she brushed away an errant tear.

Wade's expression softened, and compassion glistened in his dark eyes. A sad smile curved the well-shaped corners of his mouth as he reached up to touch her cheek. "Well"—he brushed at the streak of dirt that her thoughtless swipe at the tear had left—"it looks like I had Ice figured all wrong. I thought there was more to him than that."

A giggle born of hysteria gurgled up in Silky's throat. "You may not be wrong much, but when you are wrong, you're exceptionally wrong!"

His exhale was audible. "Especially lately." Shaking his head wearily, he offered, "Listen, Silky. Let's tell him together. Maybe if he knows that he has two friends in Anchorage who'll write, and who are interested, he'll take it better." He took her arm in a gentle grasp of reassurance. "What do you say?"

A great relief rushed through her body, making her feel as limp as a rag doll. She hadn't realized until this moment how much the pressure had been building up, knowing that she had the sole responsibility of breaking Randy's heart. Somehow, Wade made it seem less hopeless. With the beginnings of a smile that seconds ago she would never have considered possible, Silky nodded. "Yes. Thanks. I would really appreciate that."

He squeezed her arm and smiled. "Well, like they say—there's no time like the present. Why don't you, Randy and I take a little walk?" He stood, pulling her to her feet with him. "Randy has friends. We just need to make sure he believes that."

Wade still held her arm. With a grateful smile, she touched the hand there. "I wish I'd confided to you some time ago, Wade. I—" Her eyes had moved to Randy's tent. A flickering behind the nylon caught her immediate attention and her face closed in a confused grimace. Cocking her head, she asked, "Wade, does Randy have a lantern? It looks as though he has a fire—"

"God in heaven! Randy!" The high-pitched shriek of panic split the quiet evening as Ice rushed virtually through the fledgling fire he had been tending toward Randy's tent. Silky stood transfixed. She saw a small, black circle form on the nylon and grow like a cancer, as smoke began to stream upward from its center.

She felt a hard yank on her arm as Wade leapt up. "The kid's bedroll is on fire—" he growled, pulling her with him.

Before they could get there, Ice had literally torn the nylon apart with a strength she would never have imagined possible for someone of his slight build. Smoke billowed out of the torn tent, and Silky prayed, "Good Lord. Don't let him have suffocated in all that smoke."

Ice was dragging the unconscious child from his burning bedroll while Wade, Leonard and Dan were dousing the fire with damp earth. Silky ran to Ice, trying to keep panic from rising in her throat. She must keep calm. Randy's life could depend on the next few minutes.

"Ice—" she choked, "let me look at him. He may need CPR."

Ice lifted his head toward her, but he didn't seem to see or hear. He just sat there, rocking Randy's head in the crook of his arm. Silky bit her lip to see his hands, burnt and blackened. But Ice didn't seem to notice as he held Randy, smoothing back his singed hair with the underside of his free wrist. His silver glasses had been knocked away in his attempt to rescue the boy, and unheeded tears flowed freely down his sooty cheeks. He was pleading in broken sentences, "Gimme a break, will ya kid? Dammit—can't ever do anything the easy way? Ya gotta do it all wrong first—like me, like your dumb old man." He sniffed and wiped his nose with the back of his arm. "Ya gotta try to kill yourself just to prove to me what a dumb jerk I've been—"

"Ice!" Silky touched his arm carefully. He was so blackened by the soot that she couldn't be sure how serious his burns were, but she had to get his attention. "Ice. You have to let me—"

His distracted, glazed expression told her that trying to reason with him would do no good. Without waiting any longer, she bent to check Randy's pulse. It was strong, and she breathed a sigh of relief. A sharp cough from the boy riveted her attention back to his smoke-darkened, pinched and dirty face. He was breathing!

Reaching up, she loosened his shirt, checking his face with slow, professional care. He was surprisingly free of burns. His eyebrows were singed, as was the hair on the left side of his head. There was a possibility of a few first- and second-degree burns that would have to be treated and watched. But all in all, he looked pretty good.

He coughed again, stirring in Ice's arms. When he opened his eyes, they were swimming. "Da—daddy?" His raspy voice was unsure, questioning. "I'm sorry. Guess I fell asleep while I was—"

Ice nodded, quieting the boy. "I know, kid. You were smoking." With fingers that had to be in terrible pain, Ice smoothed the boy's cheek. "Tell ya what, muscle-head. You promise me you'll give up smoking and I promise I'll get us that two-bedroom apartment, so you can have that room of your own. What do you say? Deal?"

"Deal . . ." Randy squinted up at his father. "Hey, Ice. You crying?"

Ice pressed his lips together and swallowed hard, shaking his head. "Well, kid, sometimes a good cry is an important part of growing up. I suspect you'll just have to get used to it, cause I figure you and me are gonna be doing some pretty heavy growing up together."

Now Silky wasn't breathing. She stared, unblinking, at Ice as he smiled down at the boy in his arms. What had he just said? They'd be doing their growing up together? *Together!*

Randy coughed again and closed his eyes, snuggling into the smoky shirtfront that cradled him. "Looks like you need me more than I figured. . . ." Tired, but contented, he let the sentence trail away.

She felt a light tap on her shoulder, lifting her from her dreamlike trance. "Silky?" It was Leonard. "Wade and I will ride back to that last truck stop and call an ambulance. Luckily, Whitehorse is only about twenty miles down the main highway."

She nodded. "Thanks. While you're gone, I'll get these fellows bandaged up." She looked past Leonard's concerned face to see Wade standing quietly beside the charred remains of Randy's tent. His expression was solemn, waiting. Pushing herself up from the ground, she hurried to him and, without a second thought, put her arms about him, sighing happily. "Oh, Wade. They're all right." With a crack in her voice, she looked up at him. "And Ice is going to keep Randy. Can you believe it? He's going to keep him after all." With a relief she hadn't felt in weeks, she buried her face in Wade's chest, and let the relieved tears flow.

At first, Wade just stood, his expression somewhat surprised, but after a few seconds, he lifted his arms very gently to her back, holding her as a friend might hold another friend, murmuring, "I'm glad, Silky. I'm very glad."

"When did you say they'd be released from the hospital?" Annie asked, pedaling up beside Silky the next morning.

"They're both doing so well that the doctor said they'd be back in Anchorage before we are," Silky told Annie. "I got their phone number. I promised them I'd let them know when all the packs will be getting together for the 'Biked-Alaska' celebration. It ought to be some party— lots of stories."

"It should be fun—" Annie gasped, swerving wildly into the middle of the gravel road, shouting, "Watch out, Silk! That dog!"

Silky swiveled her head around to see a large,

snarling dog leap from behind the roadside trees. It growled and snapped at her front wheel, making it hard for her to keep upright. She sucked in a frightened breath, but she knew that she had to stay on her bike.

The dog jumped at the tire, its forepaws slamming down on her narrow front fender. She screamed and felt herself falling, her bike skidding sidewise on the loose gravel. The wheels slid under the dog's legs, forcing it to back away, and Silky ended up on her side in the road, one leg caught under the bike, the other dangerously open to the animal's attack.

Before she had time to right herself or try to get away, she heard the skidding of another bike. Dazed, she lifted herself up on one elbow to see Wade towering above her. He'd unfastened his water bottle from the frame of his bicycle and was squirting a stream of water into the dog's face.

Startled by the torrent, the dog dashed away, whimpering, and ran back into the woods. It had all happened so quickly, that Silky could only stare after the retreating ball of shaggy, black fur. Before she had gathered her wits enough to check herself for injury, Wade was bending over her. His face was tensed, his eyes full of concern. "Are you all right?" The whispered words were strained, and she could see a muscle jumping in his jaw.

"I—I don't know." She pushed with her forearm and sat up as Wade pulled her bicycle off of her. Grimacing, she bent her leg to try to stand.

Her hip ached, and she was pretty sure that she had scraped it badly when she landed. "Ouch."

Wade had leaned her bike against a pine tree. "The bike's okay. Now let's have a look at you."

Annie put an arm around her. "Kid, I'm so sorry. I wasn't paying attention."

Groaning, Silky let her friend take a good portion of her weight. "Me neither. It serves me right."

"Well, we'll take care of you first, then I'll shoot myself in the foot later to even things out, okay?"

Silky laughed weakly, shaking her head, but she didn't say anything as she twisted to look at her leg. Surprisingly, it was practically unscratched. But, as she suspected, her hip was scraped over a three-inch area.

"Yuck! That's some strawberry." Annie lifted her upper lip in disgust. "I'm going to be sick."

"Steady, girl. You're going to have to help me put a gauze patch on that. I can't reach it very well."

Annie sucked in her cheeks and crossed her eyes. Her exaggerated look of distress tickled Silky—until Annie spoke. "Look, doc. You want a car, I'll get you a good deal. You want your back porch patched, you call on somebody else. The sight of gauze makes me nauseous." She swallowed heavily, squinting up the empty road. Apparently no one else had noticed their mishap.

As Annie's eyes swung back to settle on Wade,

an alarm buzzer went off in Silky's brain and she stiffened, opening her mouth. But she got no further in her attempt to stop Annie's unthinkable suggestion, "Ahhh," Annie said, looking around wildly. "What about our cop friend here? He's trained in basic first aid."

Silky lifted a shaky hand to her throat, jerking her head in the negative. "No. Maybe you could go get Riva or Beth or—"

"Florence Nightingale? Come on, honey, everybody else is at least a couple of miles on down the road by now. I tell you what. I'll stand guard outside the bushes, and if either one of you starts calling for help, I'll ride up ahead and get somebody. How's that?"

Wade chuckled. "That's a load off my mind."

Silky felt like a sack emptied forcefully of its air. Glowering at them both, she ground out between clenched teeth, "You two are very funny. I hope you're never hurt and in need of my help!"

"From that look, I'd say she has a point," Annie suggested with an unbothered grin.

Wade sobered, pulling a small first aid kit from his pannier. "Let's do it, Silky. I'll be careful, I promise."

"The first time I heard that I was in the back seat of our high-school football captain's sports car." She was trying to act as though her injury wasn't painful. In truth, her hip was throbbing.

Wade lifted a well-shaped brow. "Oh?"

"Yes. He got punched."

"Look at it this way, Wade." Annie began to coax Silky forward with a hold that would have been envied by a barnacle. "At least she didn't say, '*too*.'" She handed Silky over to Wade, relinquishing her gluelike grip only when she was sure that Wade was holding her securely.

"Come on, Silky. We're friends, aren't we?" he urged with a lopsided grin.

"Sure." It was a reluctant agreement. "Thanks for your help." More to herself than to him, she murmured, "It looks like you did a better job of making a friend than I did at getting my . . ." Her mind flashed to Rex and the scene in the tent. She couldn't force herself to admit any more.

"At what?" He stopped walking and turned toward her; his face held a waiting, almost hopeful look.

"Never mind. It was nothing." She took a deep breath, closing her eyes as she limped reluctantly into the trees.

"I seriously doubt that." Taking her arm, he declared, "Some other time." Inclining his head toward a mossy area on the north side of a stand of spruce, he suggested mildly, "There's a soft-looking spot. You lie down on your stomach and—"

She interrupted. "I know how to do it, thanks."

As she lowered herself to the moss, he admitted softly, "You certainly do."

The murmured remark, with its definite sensual overtones, sent a current of unease shooting through her. Once on her stomach, she put her chin in her hands and peered sidelong over her shoulder at him. Trying to inject a degree of calm into her voice, she changed the subject. "When does our cruise ship for the Glacier Bay National Monument tour leave Juneau?"

He was opening a sterile gauze pack, preparing to put disinfectant on the open scrape. His lips twitched with humor. Her abrupt change of subject didn't fool him. Without looking up at her, he very gently lifted the hem of her shorts to expose her bare hip.

She bit her lower lip, wondering what he was thinking. Though she wanted to close her eyes and turn away, she kept her gaze trained suspiciously on his face. She watched his expression change from vague amusement to serious concentration as he tenderly began to clean the wound. Between clenched teeth, she sucked in a breath, and he stopped immediately, his eyes darting to her face.

"I'm sorry. I guess I'm pretty heavy-handed at this."

Ashamed at her display of weakness, she assured him, "It's not your fault. Go on."

Very cautiously, with more care than she had seen most medical personnel take, Wade cleansed and bandaged her hip. Before he was half-finished, she found herself relaxing, and she turned her face away, resting her head on her hands and closing her eyes. He was as gentle with her wound as he had been with her when they had made love—She started, lifting her head.

"Damn! I'm sorry, Silky." He misinterpreted her sudden move as pain. "I'm almost finished."

Biting her lip, she said nothing, waiting for him to complete the operation. "There." He smoothed her shorts down. "Need some help up?" It was a question, but he was already helping her before she had time to say anything.

Once standing, Silky tested her leg. The hip was tender, making her limp slightly. She didn't relish the fact that they still had eight hours left to ride before reaching Juneau's coast and the two-day cruise that would take them to Homer, and their final leg back to Anchorage. But she was certainly looking forward to the restful cruise—sleeping in a real bed, showering in a real bathroom, and eating at a real table.

"Okay. I've stowed the supplies." Wade stood up, tucking the first aid kit under his arm and taking her elbow. When they reached the edge of the woods, an easy laugh rumbled deep in his chest as he observed dryly, "Well, now we even walk alike."

Chapter Eleven

"L eonard and I are going to the back of the boat
and sit by the pool down on Goldrush deck." As
Annie announced her plans, Leonard helped her
from her chair in the Garden Room of the *Royal
Alaskan Lady*'s promenade deck. They had just
finished breakfast. Grabbing the last piece of
toast from her plate, she took Leonard by the
wrist and led him away. "Come, Lennie, the
glaciers await."

Silky sat back, enjoying the softness of the
leather bench seat of the booth she shared with
Rex, Riva, George and Wade. Now that Leonard
and Annie were gone, they were all shifting
around to take advantage of the extra room.
Silky was shifting for another reason, too. Her
hip was still a little tender, but she felt really

quite good after her restful night's sleep in a real bed.

They'd arrived on board last night at Juneau, and as far as she knew, everyone had gone straight to bed just as she had. While they'd slept, the *Royal Alaskan Lady* had traveled one hundred miles to reach Glacier Bay. During breakfast, the captain had announced that they would be spending a good part of the day gliding smoothly along the bay area, viewing some of the most spectacular ice floes Alaska had to offer; and Sag Pack, refreshed and relaxed, was ready to enjoy the rest of their forty-eight-hour sightseeing tour of Alaska's glacier-dotted southern coast.

She looked around at the people at her table. Wade was wearing a cotton madras short-sleeve shirt in the warm colors of summer. His slacks were khaki, topped with a web belt finished with harness-leather ends. His brown-on-brown Princeton saddle shoes had been a surprise. He seemed so—so Ivy League.

Rex was every inch the fashion model in a high-style black jumpsuit, its front zipper opened in a deep vee to reveal the thick mat of blond hair on his chest. His black suede trail boots had to be expensive, if she was any judge. And she felt that six years of marriage allowed her to be. All those years, she'd paid the bills.

George was dressed conservatively in navy wash slacks and a white pullover cotton knit shirt. It was the first time she'd seen the men all spiffed up and smelling faintly of tangy after-shaves, and it made her smile to see them looking so civilized, for a change. It had been obvious that the men felt the same way about seeing the women in dresses, considering the compliments she and the other women had received this morning. The experience had been a deviation from the norm, but a pleasant one.

Since none of them had had much space to pack for a cruise, she had brought only one dress. She was glad now that she had picked this mint green sundress. The soft, spring color brought out the mossy highlights of her eyes and enhanced the corn-silk lightness of her hair. After weeks of shorts and T-shirts, she felt an unexpected lift in looking like a woman again.

"Isn't this wonderful!" Riva gushed to no one in particular, drawing Silky's attention. Riva, too, was wearing a sundress that was well suited to her dark hair and olive skin. Her dress was of an airy, red gauze fabric that hid nothing of her considerable assets with the generously low sweep of its bodice.

She curled both of her hands around her tall orange-juice glass and lifted her chin toward the wall of windows that circled the end of the room. "Look at that glacier. It's like a frozen waterfall spilling out of the clouds. How many feet high do you think it is, Rex—three hundred?"

He turned to look out at the glistening snout of one of the sixteen active tidewater glaciers inside Glacier Bay. With a thoughtful frown, he sipped his juice. "Let's see, this ship is eight decks high—something over one hundred feet tall, and we're just one deck below the top—"

"No more than two hundred, from what I've read." Wade drew Silky's eyes as he answered Riva's question. "That's about the maximum height for these ice floes. Anyone care to join me up on deck?"

"Let's all go," Silky suggested. "It looks like we're getting pretty deep into the bay now, and we should be seeing lots more glacier activity."

Everyone in agreement, they shuffled and scooted out of the booth and headed toward the double doors on the plush, emerald-colored carpet. It was the largest lounge on the ship, dubbed the Garden Room because exotic plants of all shapes and sizes, in giant pots or hanging planters, were scattered around the high-ceilinged salon, giving one the feeling of being outdoors. Except, of course, the gentle swaying of the floor beneath their feet was a silent, ever-present reminder that they were on the sleek white queen of Alaska's cruise ships.

Silky ran her finger along the mahogany edge of a ten-foot-long planter that was a divider between the double-doored entry and the tables. She mused aloud, "I heard that when the snout of a glacier falls into the bay, it makes such immense waves they can swamp a boat."

"But not a ship." Rex laughed lightly. "Don't worry, Sil, you're in no danger."

She felt the stab of his words for what they were—a stab. He was being condescending

again. How many times had he spoken to her
this way since the Fourth of July? She'd lost
count. He obviously needed to punish her—hurt
her for hurting him, rejecting him. The truth
was, she hadn't rejected him, not really. She
just hadn't felt well.

She allowed Wade to hold the door for her as
she passed outside onto the breezy promenade
deck. The cool ocean air revived her flagging
spirits a little. Sometime during the course of
this trip, she vowed that she would get Rex
alone and talk to him.

The day passed from sunny morning to crisp,
clear night. They had cruised from Glacier Bay
deep into Lituya Bay. Silky's hair billowed and
danced about her face as she stood by the rail of
the observation deck. The breeze, sliding off the
glacier into the bay, was cold, and she hugged
herself as she and over one hundred other passengers listened to the naturalist provided by the
cruise line. Their speaker was a young, plain-
faced woman with a bright smile and an undis-
guised love for her work. Holding a microphone,
she motioned toward Lituya Glacier as the ship
began to circle around toward the mouth of
Lituya Bay. Their final destination, Homer, was
now twenty-four hours ahead.

In a softly modulated voice, the woman
pointed out the towering snout of the glacier. It
was a spectacular blue white sight in the late-
night sunset. The sky above the ice cliff blazed
red and yellow, and the fire of the extinguishing

sun was reflected all about them in the calm waters.

The scene was stunning, almost too beautiful to be disturbed by the human voice. But, Silky admitted, at least the voice was pleasant. "A severe earthquake in 1958," the woman was saying, "brought down . . ."

Against her will, Silky yawned behind her hand, shivering. It wasn't that she was bored; she wasn't. But it had been a long day, and she was getting awfully cold. The trip had been wonderful, so far, and restful, and the scenery had been spectacular. But she felt a little down, even so. She really needed to have that talk with Rex—to clear the air about a lot of things.

She looked around. Rex wasn't there. Maybe he'd already gone to bed. Good. Now might be an excellent opportunity to catch him alone. Slipping back through the crush of passengers crowded onto the observation deck, she headed for the stairs that would take her down to the promenade deck's bank of elevators.

The ride down four levels seemed to take forever. When the door finally opened, she hurried past the closed gift shop, through the empty lobby and the purser's office toward the fore cabins.

She knocked at his door. "Rex?" she whispered breathlessly. "Rex, I need to talk to you." Feeling sure that he was inside and on his way to open the door, Silky turned the knob. Pushing on the door she slipped quietly in. The overhead light was on. "Rex I—"

"Oh God!" The surprised and horrified squeal was definitely female—and familiar. Silky stood stock still as a flurry in the sheets produced first Rex, bolting up, hurriedly covering himself to the waist, and then Riva, her dark hair tangled about her face in the wild disarray of interrupted passion. Silky's insides lurched as she watched Riva cower behind the covers.

Rex's mouth worked soundlessly for a moment before he finally blurted, "Silky, what are you doing here?"

She took a step backward into the door. With her weight against it, it latched. Her throat closed as she took in the sight of her ex-husband —a man who had said he was dying for her only days ago—and the beautiful Riva Healy.

"Silky! Say something, will you? Don't just stare like an idiot!" Rex ground the words out through clenched teeth.

Silky stood there, mutely, with her hands pressed flat against the cold metal door. Seeing what she was forced to see was a torture that she wouldn't have wished on her worst enemy. Though her body had gone rigid and stony, she felt no tears, and she knew she would survive this new—this last—hurt that Rex had caused her. She'd been wrong about the importance of making her marriage work. He'd killed whatever they had had long ago, and she'd done no one any good by trying to bring it back to life.

What had Wade said to her once? Sometimes it's the marriage that is the mistake? She took a deep breath and felt a little more steady on her feet. How simple and very clear it all seemed now. The marriage had been the mistake; the divorce had been a blessing in disguise. It was funny that it always seemed to be Wade who—

"If you think the silent treatment is going to work, you're wrong, Sil. I'm a *man* and I need a *woman!* Don't forget, you turned me down. Besides, we aren't married. There are no strings tying us right now! You don't have a thing to say about this!" he lashed out in a caustic whisper. "So don't go accusing me of cheating again."

Silky inhaled deeply, lifting her chin. "Don't worry, Rex. I just came"—putting her hand on the knob, she turned it—"to say good-bye." With her shoulders back and her head held high, she turned silently and walked out of the room. As the door closed behind her, so did a chapter of her life that she had never expected to end.

"You're quite a woman. It took a lot of class to make that exit."

Her bewildered gaze ricocheted to the tall form leaning against the wall in the darkened hallway. "Wha—what are you doing here, Wade?"

"Sorry, Silky. I saw Rex and Riva leave together earlier, and when you left, too—well, I thought it wouldn't hurt for me to be handy—just in case you needed a friend." Gazing thoughtfully at her, he stepped away from the wall. "You okay?"

"Truth?" At his slow nod, she ran a weak hand through her hair, mumbling, "I feel like I've been hit by a truck."

He slid an arm about her shoulders. "Then why are you still standing?"

She flung him a distracted look, her eyes brimming with pain. "Lie down and die? No thanks, Wade. I'm no quitter."

He squeezed her shoulders and began walking with her. His deep voice was soothing, gentle. "That's what I meant." Softly stroking her hair, he said simply, "But, you have just seen the man you love in bed with someone else. You do have the right to cry if you feel like it."

The tender murmur against her ear ripped away the last, violently mutilated shreds of her pride, and she pressed her hands against her trembling lips, blinking to clear her vision. Tears of desolation stole out from beneath her closed eyes and streamed down her cheeks as she bobbed her head sadly. "Oh Wade—" she choked out in a sob. "You've been so kind."

Pulling her close, he led her toward her room. "That's what friends are for. Just tell me what you need. Would you like to talk?"

"Thanks, Wade, but, no. Not right now." She wiped at her cheek, sniffing. "I need some time alone—to think."

She could hear his low exhale as he reassuringly stroked her arm. "I understand." They'd reached her door, and he turned her to face him. His eyes were vibrant and discerning as he studied her pale face. "But remember, Silky. You aren't alone."

Chapter Twelve

*W*hat a dinner!" Annie plopped down uninvited beside Silky on the sand. "I do believe I may just have to move down here to Homer and open up a Jeep dealership, just so that I can dig clams and catch fresh crab for my dinner every night." She drew her knees up and rested her chin on one. "Speaking of dinner, honey, you should have eaten." Giving Silky a motherly stare of stern, but loving, concern, she said, "Okay, I'm here. Let's talk."

Silky had been drawing aimless pictures in the sand with a stick. She'd purposely searched out this quiet little cove to be alone, although what good it was doing to be alone continuously was anybody's guess. All the final day of the cruise, she had stayed in her room, pleading seasickness. She scraped the stick over her pensive doodling, hoping that Annie hadn't seen Wade's name scrawled over and over in the wet sand.

Dropping the stick, she turned to Annie and leaned back on her hands. "Look—I'd really rather not talk right now, if you don't mind."

"I know that." She tugged on her ear, keeping her eyes leveled on her friend. "Since when has that ever stopped me before?"

"Never." Silky sighed, lifting her eyes to scan the early-evening sky above the ocean. She squinted out across Cook Inlet toward St. Augustine, a sometimes active volcano. It was sleeping quietly now, and she envied it its peace. "What's the burning question this time?"

Annie cleared her throat, drawing Silky's eyes. "You weren't really seasick yesterday, were you?"

Silky shook her head. "I just had some thinking to do."

"Did you?"

"Did I think?" Silky shrugged. "For all the good it did me, yes."

Annie pulled on her upper lip with her teeth. "Uh. You caught Rex with Riva last night, didn't you?"

Silky felt a stab of pain in the pit of her stomach at the reminder, and she jerked her head around to stare at her friend. "My God! Did Wade tell you?"

Annie shook her head. "Did Wade know, too?

Rexie-boy isn't very subtle, is he?" Annie dropped a sympathetic hand to Silky's shoulder. "Sorry, kid. No. Wade didn't tell me. George did. Poor old sap—he was pretty drunk and needed a sturdy shoulder to cry on."

"I think I understand how he felt." Silky stood up, feeling the need to move, uncomfortable with the vivid memory of Rex and Riva together. Turning away, she wiped her hands on her shorts and began to walk toward the camp's big bonfire.

"Honey—" Silky could hear Annie shuffle to her feet. "I've always hated those goody-goody types who say 'I told you so,' but the whole reason I brought you on this trip was for you to see for yourself what a clunker that guy is." She reached over and slid a comforting arm about Silky's shoulders. "So now you know, and you've been thinking. What'd you come up with?"

Bitter amusement lifted Silky's lips with Annie's question. "Well, considering your unusual sense of humor, I think you'll get a real kick out of this." She looked out over the water to watch a sea bird swoop down to skim the ocean's surface.

Annie honored her friend's silence while she, too, watched the bird dive, but with its graceful arc skyward again, Annie planted her hands firmly on her narrow hips. "Silk, the only thing that would make me laugh right now is if you said you were gonna kick old Rexie around a couple of continents."

"No. It's not nearly so sensible as that." Dropping her eyes to the sand, Silky watched a wave recede and lose itself in the churning sea. "I'm in love with Wade Banning. I—I didn't realize it until last night when I finally knew that Rex and I were through."

"You're in love . . ." The sentence disappeared as Annie's mouth froze in a startled "oh." But, in the old Annie Toone, "grab life by the tail and hold on" fashion, she bounced right back. "You love Wade Banning?" She grabbed Silky by the wrists. "Well, give me a crystal ball and call me psychic, honey. *It worked!*"

Silky looked down at her trapped arms and then lifted her startled gaze back to Annie's radiant face. "What worked?"

"This trip, dummy. Why do you think I put you through this—I mean besides the fact that I wanted you to discover how rotten an apple Rex is?"

"I imagine it was because you're a sadist. Would you mind letting go? My hands are numb."

"Oops, sorry." She dropped Silky's arms without much notice. "Besides *that*, smart aleck! I got you here to meet Wade. I just knew you two would like each other. And God knows, you deserved to meet somebody better than Rex. Oh, I know that there really aren't any men in the world worth the space they take up. But I think Wade's better than most." She put both hands on Silky's cheeks, drawing her face up until the two women were almost nose to nose. "But you're too chicken to tell him how you feel, aren't you? That's your problem, isn't it?"

"Tell him?" Silky pulled away, running a shaky hand over her eyes. "Oh, Annie. I couldn't tell him a thing like that. He's been a friend—a good friend. Besides, he told me himself that after being rejected by his fiancée a year ago, he's only looking for friendship—not love. I'd just embarrass us both if I told him how I feel."

Annie leveled a highly skeptical look at Silky and grunted. "Men never set out looking for a wife, but when the right one comes along they all start begging to be taken home like puppies." She pointed a finger at the tip of Silky's nose. "If you want my advice, I'd say go to him and tell him you love him. You might be surprised at how he reacts to the news."

"Oh, Annie . . ." Silky wailed. "I couldn't possibly!" She spun away, unable to face her friend's pointed stare. "The man just wants to be my friend. If he was in love with me, wouldn't he have told me?"

"Okay, maybe you're right. I can do a lot of things, but I can't read men's minds." She folded her arms determinedly across her chest. "But, think, Silky. If you really love him like you say you do, you've got nothing to lose by going to him and telling him that you and Rex are *kaput*. Let him take it from there." She snorted derisively. "Men are, on the whole, dumb creatures, but I figure Wade Banning to be a good deal smarter than most."

Silky's face closed in a thoughtful frown. For a long moment there was no sound but for the rushing of the waves. Then, with a deep breath, Silky nodded determinedly. "You're right, Annie. I don't have anything to lose."

"And maybe Wade to gain." Annie slanted her a crooked smile.

Silky's mind barely caught Annie's light remark as she clutched her hands together. Suddenly her throat had completely closed. Her whole consciousness was centered on her need to find Wade and tell him that she was through with Rex, that she was a free woman—free, only if you could call the velvet chains of her love for Wade, freedom.

Annie lifted a thumbs-up, and grinned reassuringly. "You go on and find that muscle-bound cop, honey, and I bet you ten years' commissions that you'll be Mrs. Wade Banning before your sunburn heals."

"If you're right, Annie, I promise we'll name our first child after you."

Annie waved the idea away. "Heck, Silk. If I'm right, I expect you two to buy your Jeeps from me for the rest of your lives. Let the kids name themselves!" She gently shoved her friend forward. "Now go on. You have a man to catch."

With a weak smile, Silky walked away. Chewing on her lower lip, she circled the camp on leaden feet. She could see George, Riva, Rex, Leonard, Dan and Beth sitting around the roaring bonfire, roasting marshmallows. Wade wasn't there.

Scanning the beach south, toward the point, she saw him. As the sun settled low over the western horizon, it gave the impression that he was standing there nude, his legs braced wide as he faced the ocean. As she drew closer, she could see that he was wearing only his golden brown biking shorts, the color blending evenly with his tan. The sight of him made her breath catch in her throat. He had his hands clasped behind his back as he stood there, straight and strong, like a century-old pine.

A gust of wind caught his dark hair, and she had a tremendous urge to run her fingers through the soft curls that she had grown to love. He was a beautiful man, a tender and sensitive man. He was the man she loved. Only last night he had told her to tell him what she needed. But could he really give it to her once she told him that what she needed was his love? Her heart leaped with the hope that Annie was right. In fearful anticipation, she squared her shoulders.

Her breath was coming in short, nervous pants by the time she reached him, and she was feeling dangerously lightheaded. "Wade?" She could barely hear her own voice. When he didn't turn around, she tried again. "Wade?" This time he did.

She sucked in a ragged breath, trying to manufacture a calm façade. It wasn't an easy thing

to do in the face of his brooding expression.
When he realized who had called, his handsome
features softened in a smile. "Hi. I was wondering if you were ever going to join us again.
But—considering everything—I don't blame you
for not wanting to be with the group." His eyes
were steady, watching her. "Did you get your
thinking done?"

"Yes." With enormous effort, she tried for a
smile. It was a quivering failure. "I want to talk
to you. Could—we?"

He lifted his chin in a half-nod. "Sure. What
are friends for?"

There was that word—a word that could mean
so much or so little. It made her back stiffen as
she moved up to stand beside him. Motioning for
them to go on around the point, away from
camp, she croaked, "This way?"

With a nod, he placed a light hand at her back
and began to walk in the direction she indicated.
"How was dinner?" he asked conversationally.

"I—I didn't eat. Didn't you?"

"No, I took a walk." He hesitated and gazed at
her for a moment. Finally he said, "What did you
want to talk about, Silky?" The husky warmth of
his voice made her stumble to a halt. Lifting his
hand from her back to her arm, he drew her to
face him, his gaze filled with warm concern.

Clasping her hands together, she fought a
tremendous urge to reach up and touch his
handsome face. Here was a man who had never
lied to her, never asked anything of her that she

wasn't willing to give freely. He had been her friend when she'd needed one. God forbid that was all he wanted to be!

She took a deep breath, trying to build her courage. She owed him the truth. After all he'd done for her, all he'd been, he deserved to know how she felt—and now was the time to tell him. She worked hard at meeting his eyes. Deep within the vital darkness, she drew her courage. "Wade—" she began.

"*Silky!*" Rex's shout intruded, and they both turned to see him trotting down the beach, waving. "*Hey, Silky.* Where've you been? I've got to talk to you!" He caught up to them and slid an arm about her shoulders. "Say, Banning." He cocked his head as though he were directing Wade to leave. "You don't mind, do you? This is important."

The expression that came over Wade's face was strained. With a quick, appraising glance at Silky, he asked. "Would you like me to stay?"

Yes, oh yes she would! She wanted him to stay forever. But there was something else she wanted, too. And that was to make sure that Rex knew once and for all that she no longer had any interest in seeing him or hearing his voice—or even his name ever again! With a slow shake of her head, she answered, "It's all right, Wade. Rex and I need to have this talk."

He nodded, his long lashes lifting to take in Rex's tall frame. "Whatever you say." Without another word, he turned away to limp back toward the camp. Silky watched him go with her heart blocking her throat, completely forgetting Rex and the fact that his arm was slung heavily across her shoulders. When he spoke, she jumped with surprise.

"Sil, darling—"

She hissed, "Don't call me darling! Never, *never* again in your life, Rex, dare to call me that!" She twisted out from under his arm and pushed him away. "Now! Just what do you think we could possibly have to discuss?"

"Please, Silvia. Let me explain about what happened with Riva and me."

"Rex, I don't care if Riva forced you into bed at gunpoint! The women you—you entertain simply don't matter to me anymore."

She watched as his light eyes grew wide. "You don't mean that," he pleaded hoarsely.

A sad, soft laugh gurgled up in her throat. "I've never meant anything more, Rex." Lifting her hand to his cheek, she patted it as though he were a puppy. Silky somehow knew that this would be her last moment alone with Rex, and she was thankful that it hurt no more than it did. "Good luck, Rex." Withdrawing her hand, she turned away. "Now, if you'll excuse me, I have to see a man about buying Jeeps—for the rest of his life."

"Didn't go last night, did it?" Annie asked in a low whisper as Silky drank from her water bottle.

Silky swallowed hard. "No, it didn't. Whose idea was it to go on that seashell hunt until all hours? I finally dragged myself to bed at one o'clock, without ever having a chance to get Wade alone."

"Tough luck, Silk." Annie squirted water on her face. "I think the hunt was George's idea. My guess is he figured little Riva couldn't stray very far if everybody was together and out in the open."

Silky sighed and fastened her bottle to the bike frame. "Well, everybody was sure together! Annie, I'm going crazy—"

Annie put her fingers to Silky's lips. "Nix the chatter, kiddo. Wade's coming down the line. I guess this nasty head wind has finally gotten to him. "Hey, Wade?" She waved gaily.

He waved back, smiling. As he moved toward them, Silky noticed how badly he was limping, and her heart cried out to take him in her arms and comfort him. She forced her gaze to drift away, across the highway, to the cool green waters of Cook Inlet. With a finger of the Pacific stretching inland on her left, and the grand beauty of the Kenai Wildlife Refuge on her right, Silky was sorry that her mood was not more receptive to nature's artistry.

Tightening her safety helmet strap, Annie quipped, "Say Wade, if Rexie's going to lead us, do you mind if I hold us up a minute to take out additional accident insurance?"

Silky felt a sweet stab at the sound of Wade's deep chuckle as Rex called back over his shoulder, "I heard that, Toone. If you don't like the way I do it, then you just get your tail up here and take over."

"You got a deal, Overbridge. Just don't start whining about the pace I set." With that, she hopped on her bike and pushed on the pedal, heading up to the lead position.

One after another, Sag Pack left the roadside to battle the head wind on the last leg of their month-long trip through summertime Alaska. Silky had already situated her foot into the toe clip on her pedal and was about to push off when she noticed movement out of the corner of her eye. Turning, she realized that Wade had pulled his bike off the road into a small clearing and was taking off his helmet.

"What are you doing?" she called.

His dark gaze touched her for only a moment before he turned away to hook his helmet over his handlebars. "Still want to talk?"

Lifting her foot out of the toe clip, she wheeled her bike into the trees to stand it beside his. "It's your leg, isn't it?" There was concern in her voice. "This wind has been terrible on you, I know."

He shrugged. "Comes with the territory." As he spoke, he lowered himself to the ground and leaned tiredly against the massive trunk of a towering hemlock. "You haven't answered my question."

She settled down beside him as he started to massage his calf. Reaching out, she placed her fingers on his wrist. "Yes, I do want to talk to you." The slight touch brought his massaging to a complete halt. He didn't look up at her, but she knew that she had his undivided attention. "Once you stopped to wait with me while I rested on the side of the road. Remember?"

He lifted his eyes to her. The long lashes were lowered over a glittering blackness that made her heart thud heavily into her ribs. "I remember."

She sat back against the hard trunk, exhaling. "Remember what I said then—about cops not being poetic?"

"Vaguely." He shifted his broad shoulders so that he faced her more directly. "Why?"

She ran a hand across her face. How long ago that seemed. How very much she had learned about people—people she thought she knew like Rex and Annie; people she thought she'd figured out like Ice and Wade. Good God! Even herself! How little she'd known then, and how little she still knew. But every bit of knowledge was a step toward learning. At least she hoped so.

Her laugh was shallow and embarrassed. "Oh, I don't know. I guess I just wanted to ask you to try not to hold it against me. I'm a slow learner, but I'm—"

"No quitter? I know." His grin had a melancholy twist as he bent to massage his leg again.

It always amazed Silky that such a vast land could be so silent. Right now, it was deafeningly so. Wade wasn't going to say anything else. Apparently, he planned to let her do the talking.

She cleared her throat in an attempt to appear at least partially composed, but her stomach was in a knot, and her hands had begun to tremble. She clutched them together in her lap to hide her unease.

Things weren't going too well. Just when she needed all the strength she could muster, she felt like her insides were turning to mush. Finally, she decided that it was now or never. "Wade?" Her voice was an octave too high, and she cleared her throat.

He quit massaging his calf. With an expression of solemn curiosity he leaned toward her. "What's on your mind, Silky?"

His face was now only inches from her own, and her heart began a wild hammering that almost unbalanced her. Unclasping her hands with a great effort, she lowered them to the grass, clutching to keep from toppling into him. She felt ridiculous—like a paper clip being drawn to a magnet.

Draping an arm around his bent knee, he cocked a curious brow at her. "Why are you so nervous? I thought we were friends. Talk to me, Silky."

"*Yes!* Yes, we're friends. That's true," she managed heavily, grasping onto the straw like it was a lifeboat. "And because we're friends, I want you to promise me that when we hit the road again you'll ride in my wind shadow. I've gotten stronger on this trip, and there's no sense in my not giving a friend a hand."

He regarded her closely. "Yes. You have gotten stronger. And thanks." He reached over and touched her cheek. "Silky, listen—"

She pulled away from the warm caress of his fingers, unsnapping her helmet and tossing it to the ground. "Wade. I have something to say, and it's not going to be easy." Trying to appear all business, she cleared her throat again. Dreading his reaction to her next statement, she abruptly stood, brushing her hands on her shorts. "If you feel the urge to laugh, or anything, I won't blame you. But if you don't mind, I think I'll—I'll walk a few feet away. I'd rather not see your face."

Steadying herself against a pine trunk, she turned away from him before walking into a thicket filled with forget-me-nots. Their light fragrance wafting up was a pleasant surprise, and she took a deep breath. "I—" She clutched her fists together at her breasts, exhaling rapidly. "I—"

The words caught like dry weeds in her throat, and before she could say "love you," her knees gave way completely, and she sat down abruptly on the carpet of tiny blue flowers. "Oh God, Wade—what I'm trying to say—"

"What, darling? What do you want to tell me?" His voice was so near that she could feel the rush of air from his lips feather the fine hair at her temple. She didn't turn. She didn't speak. She only held her breath, paralyzed by his sudden nearness.

With a low groan, he took her arm, turning her around. As she watched, she was amazed to see his eyes fill with tears. "Don't dare tell me you're taking Rex back! After all you've been through—after all he's done to you! Don't say that to me—not to me!"

High emotion glistened like damp leaves in her eyes. She had no idea how beautiful a man's tears could be. "Rex? No, Wade. Rex and I are through. I told him so last night."

"Through?" He was bending down—on one knee, his sparkling eyes staring at her with a desperate intensity.

"But—but that's not what I wanted to say, Wade," she stuttered. He started to speak, but she put her fingers over his mouth. "I know you said you only wanted women for friends, and I'm sorry. I'm really sorry. I mean—" She lifted her chin with the poise of a princess about to be beheaded. "But—Wade. I'm afraid I've fallen in love with you."

"You're afraid you've . . ." The words trailed off as the truth of her statement hit him, and he raised his face to the sky, closing his eyes as though he were thanking providence for an answered prayer. A devastating smile revealed his strong, white teeth. It was a smile that cleansed her soul and made her heart leap with new hope. It was a good smile, a kind smile, a smile of love. It was the most beautiful sight she had ever seen, and ever hoped to see.

"At last," he whispered. When he opened his

eyes again, they glittered darkly with masculine decision. "Thank God." With both hands on her, he settled her down into the flowers.

His deep voice was unsteady and filled with emotion. "Silky, when a man finds himself in love with a woman who's trying to get her ex-husband back, there isn't much else he can offer her but his friendship."

"Love?" Unable to believe her own ears, she repeated the word in an awed whisper.

"Yes, love." He pressed her down into the fragrant cushion of flowers and took possession of her lips with a divine hunger, muttering unevenly against the torrid moistness of their kiss. "I'd nearly lost hope that you could give up your old dream for a new one." He pulled at her lip, moaning with her pliant response. "The decision to do that had to be yours. No matter how badly I wanted to tell you how I felt, I've learned that love can't be forced."

"I know. . . ." she whispered, a smile gentling her throbbing lips. "It can't be forced, or bought —or even chosen. . . ." She sighed as his tongue feathered the sensitive hollow at her throat.

"Only treasured," he murmured, hard promise enriching the deep timbre of his voice. Slipping her shirt up, he nuzzled her breasts. "I will always treasure your love—and the way you told me about it." His lips, his reassuring endearments and his potent body sent her emotions reeling with the startling depths of his passion, and she luxuriated in the taste and feel of him.

As they came together in mutual adoration,

she made him a silent vow. Wade would always have a wind shadow in her love. And she knew in her heart that she would have one too. They would be strong for each other, and they would be protected by each other. They could be vulnerable in each other's arms because their hearts were held in trust.

Silhouette Special Edition. Romances for the woman who expects a little more out of love.

If you enjoyed this book, and you're ready for more great romance

…get 4 romance novels FREE when you become a Silhouette Special Edition home subscriber.

Act now and we'll send you four exciting Silhouette Special Edition romance novels. They're our gift to introduce you to our convenient home subscription service. Every month, we'll send you six new passion-filled Special Edition books. Look them over for 15 days. If you keep them, pay just $11.70 for all six. Or return them at no charge.

We'll mail your books to you two full months *before they are available anywhere else.* Plus, with every shipment, you'll receive the Silhouette Books Newsletter absolutely free. *And with Silhouette Special Edition there are never any shipping or handling charges.*

Mail the coupon today to get your four free books—and more romance than you ever bargained for.

Silhouette Special Edition

MORE ROMANCE FOR
A SPECIAL WAY TO RELAX

$2.25 each

79 ☐ Hastings	105 ☐ Sinclair	131 ☐ Lee	157 ☐ Taylor
80 ☐ Douglass	106 ☐ John	132 ☐ Dailey	158 ☐ Charles
81 ☐ Thornton	107 ☐ Ross	133 ☐ Douglass	159 ☐ Camp
82 ☐ McKenna	108 ☐ Stephens	134 ☐ Ripy	160 ☐ Wisdom
83 ☐ Major	109 ☐ Beckman	135 ☐ Seger	161 ☐ Stanford
84 ☐ Stephens	110 ☐ Browning	136 ☐ Scott	162 ☐ Roberts
85 ☐ Beckman	111 ☐ Thorne	137 ☐ Parker	163 ☐ Halston
86 ☐ Halston	112 ☐ Belmont	138 ☐ Thornton	164 ☐ Ripy
87 ☐ Dixon	113 ☐ Camp	139 ☐ Halston	165 ☐ Lee
88 ☐ Saxon	114 ☐ Ripy	140 ☐ Sinclair	166 ☐ John
89 ☐ Meriwether	115 ☐ Halston	141 ☐ Saxon	167 ☐ Hurley
90 ☐ Justin	116 ☐ Roberts	142 ☐ Bergen	168 ☐ Thornton
91 ☐ Stanford	117 ☐ Converse	143 ☐ Bright	169 ☐ Beckman
92 ☐ Hamilton	118 ☐ Jackson	144 ☐ Meriwether	170 ☐ Paige
93 ☐ Lacey	119 ☐ Langan	145 ☐ Wallace	171 ☐ Gray
94 ☐ Barrie	120 ☐ Dixon	146 ☐ Thornton	172 ☐ Hamilton
95 ☐ Doyle	121 ☐ Shaw	147 ☐ Dalton	173 ☐ Belmont
96 ☐ Baxter	122 ☐ Walker	148 ☐ Gordon	174 ☐ Dixon
97 ☐ Shaw	123 ☐ Douglass	149 ☐ Claire	175 ☐ Roberts
98 ☐ Hurley	124 ☐ Mikels	150 ☐ Dailey	176 ☐ Walker
99 ☐ Dixon	125 ☐ Cates	151 ☐ Shaw	177 ☐ Howard
100 ☐ Roberts	126 ☐ Wildman	152 ☐ Adams	178 ☐ Bishop
101 ☐ Bergen	127 ☐ Taylor	153 ☐ Sinclair	179 ☐ Meriwether
102 ☐ Wallace	128 ☐ Macomber	154 ☐ Malek	180 ☐ Jackson
103 ☐ Taylor	129 ☐ Rowe	155 ☐ Lacey	181 ☐ Browning
104 ☐ Wallace	130 ☐ Carr	156 ☐ Hastings	182 ☐ Thornton

Silhouette Special Edition

$2.25 each

183 ☐ Sinclair	190 ☐ Wisdom	197 ☐ Lind	204 ☐ Eagle
184 ☐ Daniels	191 ☐ Hardy	198 ☐ Bishop	205 ☐ Browning
185 ☐ Gordon	192 ☐ Taylor	199 ☐ Roberts	206 ☐ Hamilton
186 ☐ Scott	193 ☐ John	200 ☐ Milan	207 ☐ Roszel
187 ☐ Stanford	194 ☐ Jackson	201 ☐ Dalton	208 ☐ Sinclair
188 ☐ Lacey	195 ☐ Griffin	202 ☐ Thornton	209 ☐ Ripy
189 ☐ Ripy	196 ☐ Cates	203 ☐ Parker	210 ☐ Stanford

SILHOUETTE SPECIAL EDITION, Department SE/2
1230 Avenue of the Americas
New York, NY 10020

Please send me the books I have checked above. I am enclosing $_____
(please add 75¢ to cover postage and handling. NYS and NYC residents please
add appropriate sales tax). Send check or money order—no cash or C.O.D.'s
please. Allow six weeks for delivery.

NAME _____

ADDRESS _____

CITY _____ STATE/ZIP _____

Silhouette Special Edition

Enjoy romance and passion, larger-than-life...

Now, thrill to 4 Silhouette Intimate Moments novels (a $9.00 value)— ABSOLUTELY FREE!

If you want more passionate sensual romance, then Silhouette Intimate Moments novels are for you!

In every 256-page book, you'll find romance that's electrifying...involving... and intense. And now, these larger-than-life romances can come into your home every month!

4 FREE books as your introduction.

Act now and we'll send you four thrilling Silhouette Intimate Moments novels. They're our gift to introduce you to our convenient home subscription service. Every month, we'll send you four new Silhouette Intimate Moments books. Look them over for 15 days. If you keep them, pay just $9.00 for all four. Or return them at no charge.

We'll mail your books to you *as soon as they are published.* Plus, with every shipment, you'll receive the Silhouette Books Newsletter absolutely free. *And Silhouette Intimate Moments is delivered free.*

Mail the coupon today and start receiving Silhouette Intimate Moments. Romance novels for women...not girls.

Silhouette Intimate Moments

Silhouette Intimate Moments™
120 Brighton Road, P.O. Box 5020, Clifton, NJ 07015

☐ **YES!** Please send me FREE and without obligation, 4 exciting Silhouette Intimate Moments romance novels. Unless you hear from me after I receive my 4 FREE books, please send me 4 new Silhouette Intimate Moments novels to preview each month. I understand that you will bill me $2.25 each for a total of $9.00 — with no additional shipping, handling or other charges. **There is no minimum number of books to buy and I may cancel anytime I wish.** The first 4 books are mine to keep, even if I never take a single additional book.

☐ Mrs. ☐ Miss ☐ Ms. ☐ Mr.   **BMSL24**

Name	(please print)
Address	Apt. #
City ( )	State Zip
Area Code Telephone Number	

Signature (if under 18, parent or guardian must sign)

This offer, limited to one per household, expires June 30, 1985. Terms and prices are subject to change. Your enrollment is subject to acceptance by Simon & Schuster Enterprises.

Silhouette Intimate Moments is a service mark and trademark of Simon & Schuster, Inc.